Space Trap

10

Space Trap

Monica Hughes

A Groundwood Book
Douglas & McIntyre
Toronto/Vancouver/Buffalo

Groundwood Books / Douglas & McIntyre
585 Bloor Street West
Toronto, Ontario M6G 1K5

The publisher gratefully acknowledges the assistance of the Canada
Council and the Ontario Arts Council.

Canadian Cataloguing in Publication Data

Hughes, Monica, 1925-
    Space trap

ISBN 0-88899-202-5 (pbk.)

PS8565.U43S62   jC813'.54   C83-098387-2
PZ7.H83Sp

Cover illustration by Maureen Paxton
Printed and bound in Canada

Contents

1

The Thorn Bush

It began with a game of hide-and-seek, and that would never have happened either if Valerie hadn't lost her temper.

"I'm sick and tired of babysitting Susan every day of this vacation. I haven't had a moment to myself. It just isn't fair!"

Mother ran a hand through her hair and stared at her. "But, Valerie, I'm counting on you. I've got a mass of figures for the computer and I'll never catch up with her underfoot. She won't be any trouble, will you, Susan?"

Susan shook her head and nodded and looked solemnly up at Valerie's furious face. Her thumb went into her mouth. "You see," Mother went on. "Good as gold. And what else would you do today anyway?"

Valerie glared. The infuriating thing was that Mother was right. There wasn't anything special to do on DeePeeThree, except go out on soil testing expeditions with Father, and he was bound to take Frank again. Frank got to do all the exploring. It wasn't fair. Sometimes she felt that being the middle person in the family was too much to bear.

Frank bossed her and got all the fun of field trips with Father, and Susan got spoiled by everyone and she had to look after her. Valerie gave a huge sniff and bolted to the bathroom.

When she had had a good cry, she washed her face in the

teacupful of water that the dispenser grudgingly trickled into the portable basin and stared at her tear-splotched face in the mirror.

"What an ugly skinny beast you are," she told her reflection. "No wonder nobody likes you." She thought grudgingly of Frank, who was tall, handsome and always, it seemed, in charge of his fate; and she thought of Susan, whose fair curly hair and enormous blue eyes made grown-ups croon over her until Valerie felt sick.

"I hate them. It just isn't fair." She leaned against the bathroom partition and imagined a world in which there was only Mother and Father and herself, Valerie Josephine Spencer, the most beautiful girl in the whole Federated Galaxy, long blonde hair, large blue eyes with lashes you could really notice, and a figure that went in and out, instead of being like a twig.

As always she came out of her dream feeling horribly guilty. "I don't really wish they weren't there," she told God or whoever was listening. "It's just that life's so horribly unfair."

Really, Valerie, the better half of her mind argued back to the snarky half, Mother and Father didn't have to bring you on this field trip. They could have left you back on Eden, spending the whole summer holidays in school. That happened to lots of University kids whose parents went out on Planet Changing Expeditions.

"You're lucky to be here at all," she told her reflection firmly and went back to the main part of the Expedition's tent to apologize.

Mother beat her to it. "I *am* sorry, Val. You're quite right. I've been taking you for granted quite shamelessly. Frank should do his share."

"Oh, come on, Mum." Frank's voice was as deep as Father's. He stroked his new moustache. "I'm a bit old for babysitting, don't you think? Anyway Dad and I plan to go up-country today. I mean this is good stuff, really useful for school, isn't it, Dad?"

Father nodded, not really listening. He had his coffee cup in his left hand and his right hand checked off the list he'd spread across the table. Valerie felt herself starting to boil again. In just a minute she was going to start screaming, at Frank, at Father for not paying attention when it was important, at the whole world.

Before she could blow up, Mother intervened. "You've been out with your father every day so far, Frank, and Val hasn't had a minute to herself. This is the Thirty Second century, after all. Women have some rights. Today you're going to have to look after Susan for a change and Val shall have a day off."

Valerie looked at Father, longing for him to say, "Why don't you come with me, Val? You'd be a real help."

But he just pushed back his chair, picked up his papers and said, "Well, I'm off."

She opened her mouth to ask him if she could go and then shut it again. She stood and watched him leave the tent. She listened to the whine of the floater's engine warming up. Go on, run out and ask him. He might say 'yes'. But she wouldn't ask because she was afraid that he'd say she'd only be in the way.

"Come on, Susan," said Frank in a put-on jolly voice. "Let's go and find some fun." He glared at Valerie, swung Susan onto his shoulders and galloped off with her screaming happily and kicking his chest with her feet.

Just Mum and me, thought Valerie. Perhaps she'll spend the day with me and we can talk and share feelings, woman to woman, sort of... But Mother just swept the breakfast things away and turned to the computer console that filled one wall of the living part of the big tent. "Enjoy your day off, love," she said over her shoulder and began punching keys. Well, I might as well talk to the wall, Valerie thought bitterly and drifted outside.

What *was* she going to do by herself for a whole day? Being with Father was what she'd really wanted all along. Like Frank. But he was in High School and she was still only in Primary and didn't know the first thing about Planetary Reconstruction. I'd have just been in his way, she thought gloomily. That's why he zoomed off in a hurry without waiting for me to ask if I could go too.

She scuffed through the grey dust and sat down on a grey pudding-shaped boulder. Really, this is the dullest looking planet I've ever seen, and I was twelve on July 12, 3114 and I've been planet-hopping every summer since I was as old as Susan. That makes seven years, since she's five. The planet was so dull it didn't even have a name yet. The Federation called it Delta Parvonis Three, which just meant that it was the third planet of Delta Parvonis, a rotten little sun that barely kept the planet warm enough to be comfortable.

Valerie looked across the grey plain at the distant grey mountains, and kicked her heels against the grey rock. About two hundred metres away Frank was helping Susan climb the one hill, which really wasn't a hill at all but a pile of squarish rocks almost like a pyramid, all intergrown with wiry grey brush. Susan was screaming with laughter as Frank hauled her up from rock to rock. It would be fun to join in. But she couldn't really, not after making all that fuss about wanting to have some peace on her own.

She listened to the laughter and stared at the boring greyness of DeePeeThree. Maybe it would be more interesting if she were a scientist. Perhaps she would be one when she grew up. Maybe she'd be famous, the first person to develop a large-scale matter-transmitter that really worked. They'd give her the Nobel Prize. She imagined the crowds cheering and her acceptance speech: "It was nothing really ..."

Frank and Susan were making so much noise that she just

had to turn round and see what they were up to. They were at the summit of the pyramid and Susan was on Frank's shoulders, pointing at something, she couldn't see what. Then they scrambled down to the plain and galloped off towards the old thorn thicket and vanished out of sight around the far side. After a while she couldn't hear their voices any more. In fact it was so quiet you could have heard an insect chirp, if there'd been any insects on DeePeeThree.

She strolled casually over to the hill and began to climb it herself. The blocks were almost as square as if they'd been shaped and put there by people, which was nonsense, because nothing and nobody had ever lived on DeePeeThree. The wiry brush growing in the crevices scratched her wrists and ankles. By the time she was half-way up she wondered why she was bothering. But Frank had climbed it. What he could do she could too. She struggled on and scrambled triumphantly to her feet on the topmost block, covered with grey grit and with two broken finger nails.

It had better be worth it, she thought, turning around to see the view. But it wasn't. The same grey landscape she knew and hated at ground level. What a waste of time! Then she noticed the thorn thicket. How very peculiar! From up here you could see that it wasn't just any old thicket, but it had been deliberately planted in a perfect circle. Which didn't make any sense at all, because who could have planted it?

It was unnaturally quiet. It wasn't like Susan to be quiet for this long. Unless they were playing hide-and-seek behind the thorn hedge. That's it, she told herself, as she began the climb down. In just a minute Frank will 'find' Susan and she'll scream and everything'll be ordinary again.

She slithered the last few metres to the ground. There

still wasn't a sound. Perhaps they're waiting for *me* to find them, she thought, suddenly happy. Perhaps that's the game. She ran across the dusty plain to the thicket. After all, she told herself, if Susan wants me to play I can't disappoint her just because it's my day off.

She began to walk around the perimeter of the thicket. On the far side there was a gap, like an entrance, but when she peeked in all she could see was more hedge. She ran all the way around the outside of the thicket and back to the entrance. No sign of Frank or Susan.

How quiet it was! The dry thorn bushes crackled briefly. Was that a small stifled giggle or had she imagined it? "I see you," she called out, and her voice sounded very small in the grey indifferent silence. "I'm coming to get you," she threatened. She listened. A thorn rasped across the sleeve of her blue jumpsuit and she started. How loudly her heart was beating! Silly, she told herself. It's only a game of hide-and-seek. She stepped through the opening. Ahead of her was a wall of thorn-bush, but to left and right a passage curved out of sight. She turned briskly to the right. When an opening appeared in the inside wall of the thorn bush she took it, and found she was facing yet another wall, with passages curving away to left and right.

What was going on? Then a memory clicked in her mind. It was a maze, like the ones she'd read about in ancient Europe back on Earth. They went round and round with openings leading in to the secret centre. But only one way would actually get you there. Every other passage would come to a dead end, or lead you back to a passage already explored so you went round in a circle.

This was more like it! She could bet that Frank and Susan had already found the way to the secret centre and were waiting there for her right now. She looked for foot-prints in the grey dust. There were scuff marks everywhere as Susan had run to and fro, but there wasn't a definite track to follow.

Never mind. I'll take alternate left and right turns and see what happens, she told herself. Come on, Val, show them!

It worked beautifully at first and she had penetrated four of the hedge rings before she came to a dead-end and had to turn back. She was getting warm and was awfully thirsty. It must be nearly lunch-time. But Frank and Susan were still waiting for her at the centre. She had to go on.

She broke off a thorn, a wicked silver thing ten centimetres long, and made an X in the middle of the passage. There. I'll know not to try that way again. As she straightened up she saw, marked on the trunk of a thorn bush, a strange sign.

$$\underline{\underline{111}}$$

It seemed to have been burned into the wood. It was like no Galactic script Valerie had seen before. Frank couldn't have made it. So who had? Who else had discovered the secret of the maze? On this empty planet?

She felt cold and shivered suddenly. She looked up to see if a cloud had covered the sun. But of course the cloud was always there, and it really wasn't cold at all. She was just letting her imagination run away with her, thinking that around the next bend, or the turning after that, there would be a *something* waiting ready to jump out on her.

She swallowed and told herself not to be stupid. The whole surface of DeePeeThree had been scanned before they had landed. The instruments said that without the shadow of a doubt there was nothing that ran or wriggled or bit. No animal nor reptile nor bird nor insect. Maybe some microbes, but nothing larger than that.

Valerie stuck her hands in her pockets and whistled as she walked along, keeping up her courage. The path swooped from left to right, sometimes going halfway round the circle before admitting her to an inner passage. She marked each dead-end with her thorn and glimpsed again the mysterious marking:

$$\underline{\underline{111}}$$

She'd been in this place ages. How was Frank keeping Susan quiet all this time? It was more than she'd ever been able to do.

The quality of light changed and she realised that just beyond where she stood was the centre of the maze. She'd done it! She crept along the final passage. Then with a triumphant BOO! she leapt into the open centre of the maze. Only Frank and Susan weren't there, surprised that she'd made it. There was nothing but the grey dusty ground surrounded by the tight circle of thorn hedge with one opening in it, the one through which she had come.

The hedge was so tall she could see nothing above it but grey sky, with the noon sun shimmering through it. The shimmer hurt her eyes and she wondered if she were starting a headache.

"Frank! Susan! Oh, come on. Where are you? It's not funny. Game's ooo..."

In the middle of her yell the ground seemed to fall away from under her with a suddenness that punched the breath out of her body. Then all the lights went out.

2

The Market

There was a blackness with no space and time, no breath and no heartbeat. Then in a giddy whirl they were all back again, and Valerie's mouth was open and she could hear herself screaming.

She opened her eyes and then she couldn't scream, because her throat had shrunk into a hard knot the way it does during a nightmare. That's it, she told herself. This is just a particularly horrid dream. I'm going to pinch myself and then I'll wake up in bed in the tent with Susan snoring next to me. She pinched herself very hard in the soft part of her arm, hard enough to make the tears come to her eyes, but she didn't wake up.

She was crouching on the floor of a cage, no more than a metre high and wide, so that there was barely even room to sit comfortably. The cage swayed from side to side and sometimes lurched up and down as well, because it seemed to be on the back of a truck, or something like a truck. The way she was sitting, she could see where they had come from and the road unwinding from beneath like a shiny purple ribbon.

Shiny? Purple? There were no roads like that on DeePeeThree. There were no roads at all. And she certainly wasn't back home on Eden. Ugly plants like cabbages, each the size of a house, hurtled by as the truck lurched and swayed. They were planted on each side of the road like shade trees and they gave off a nasty smell like very old cheese.

Oh, where am I? What's happening to me? She looked through the bars of her cage. The sky above was dark blue, but the horizon behind the mountains was tinged with red, as if the sun were about to rise. Overhead a white point of light shone as bright as a nova. This is a binary system and that's the second sun, she told herself cleverly. They'd just taken binary systems in Grade Five Astronomy.

Then she went cold all over. A binary system? What am I doing on a strange planet with cabbage trees and twin suns? And *how* am I ever going to get back?

She crouched at the bottom of the cage with her arms around her knees and thought about Mum and Dad on DeePeeThree goodness knows how many parsecs away. Mum would have programmed the computer to her satisfaction by now, and Dad would be coming in with the floater piled high with soil samples. Frank and Susan would rush into the tent demanding dinner and they'd all sit down to eat.

How long would it be before they missed her? She imagined them beginning to search. Realizing that she really wasn't there. She could just see Susan crying for her Val, and Frank saying it was all his fault for hiding from her in the maze. This picture comforted her for a little while, but not for long. She was cold and hungry and scared, and she'd much rather be home, even if she had to babysit every single day of her life, than be alone *here* — wherever here was. Then a really horrid thought hit her. Maybe I've gone mad and none of this is really happening at all! She hugged her knees to her chest and put her head down and cried.

After a time she stopped crying and looked up. Things were changing. A bright yellow road intersected the purple one over which she was being driven. Then another. They were passing houses now, set back from the road among the smelly cabbage trees, perfectly enormous houses, solid and clumsy looking. Her heart thumped painfully. Soon she would be seeing whatever kind of people lived on this strange twin-sunned planet. Would they be friendly? This cage wasn't friendly, but perhaps it was a mistake and when she explained...

The trees stopped and more yellow roads criss-crossed the purple. The houses were close together now, though there was still a ribbon of dull-coloured grass between each, and bushes with thick flesh-coloured blobs on them that could be flowers, but looked more like funguses.

The truck shot down the purple road and rocked to a stop in a large square paved with purple and yellow blocks. A sudden metallic sound above her head made her duck, but it was only a chain with a hook on its end that swayed and caught the bars above her head. The cage was swung into the air and dropped at the end of a line of similar cages with a jolt that left her breathless. With a squeal the truck shot off. As it left she saw on the side panel a symbol that she had seen before:

$$\underline{\underline{111}}$$

The same symbol that had been on the thorn bush in the maze on DeePeeThree. What could it all mean? What was the possible connection? She couldn't begin to think of an answer, so she wriggled carefully around in her cage until she could see her neighbour in the next cage. It was a very large furry creature, its black domed head sunk on its chest in an attitude of complete despair.

"Oh, you poor thing," she exclaimed and slid one hand through the bars of their cages to touch its fur.

"I wouldn't do that if I were you," a small dry voice spoke in Intergalactic from somewhere the other side of the furry creature.

"Oh, why?"

"Because it happens to be a *wallaroon* from Medinia, that's why." The precise voice used the Intergalactic word for 'man-eating ape-creature', and Valerie drew her hand back quickly.

"Who are you?" she asked, scrunching herself into the farthest corner of her cage away from the wallaroon, still sunk in sleep or depression, she couldn't tell which. She wasn't able to see the person who had spoken, but his voice sounded quite friendly.

"My name is Isnek Ansnek and I am from Ilenius."

"How do you do?" Valerie replied politely. "I'm Valerie Spencer from Federation Capital Eden."

"My goodness, they actually snatched you from *there*?" The dry voice was surprised.

Valerie explained about the holidays and about her parents working on DeePeeThree, which the Federation authorities on Eden thought might be engineered into a more livable planet. "But what did you mean 'snatched'?"

"Well, you obviously didn't just fall here. Any more than the rest of us. These people must be members of an outlaw planet engaged in contraband animal trading."

"Animal trading? But...but we're not animals. They'll send us back, won't they?"

"I wouldn't count on it," the distant voice said drily.

Not get back? Valerie felt exactly as if she had a block of ice in the middle of her stomach. Mr Ansnek was silent.

"Are you still there?" Her voice wavered. "How did you get here?"

"Unfortunately I am still here. I became aware of an intermittent variable light phenomenon when on a field trip into a remote area of Betnik. Upon investigating, I entered some kind of space warp and found myself a prisoner here."

Valerie thought about this. "Oh. What happened to me

was the light shimmered and then I was here instead of on DeePeeThree."

"Exactly what I said."

"Please, Mr Ansnek, what do you think they're going to do with us?"

"I would assume that most of you are destined for a collection and display facility. I believe you call it a 'zoo'. As for myself, I regret that I can see no future but disintegration."

"What do you *mean*?"

"They'll probably take me apart," the voice said drily.

Valerie hugged her knees to her chest and shivered. How could he be so calm about such a fate? Even though she had never seen him, he spoke Intergalactic and he seemed friendly. She could even imagine how he must look — rather like Mr McReady, the local minister back home on Eden, stick-dry and bony but very kind indeed.

"Oh dear," she said softly and tears began to run down her cheeks. To be in a zoo. Or to be taken apart. What a terrible choice of futures!

Oh, Mummy, I wish you were here, she thought desperately. And then: no, I don't, because you'd be in a cage too. I just wish I were home. I'd never complain or be mean to Susan or hide Frank's books or fuss over loading the dishwasher. If only this would turn out not to be real. *Please*.

She squeezed her eyes shut and held her breath. But no matter how she willed it not to be, she could still feel the cold bars of the cage and smell the unpleasant cheesy fungus smell. The wallaroon suddenly awoke and shook the bars of its cage, stamping its feet and swaying from side to side.

The sky had been getting lighter for some time now, and suddenly the big orange sun popped up above the houses to her left. As if at a signal the square began to fill with people. *People*? thought Valerie, and shrank as far back in her cage as she could. She'd seen many strange beings back on Eden, but never any like these.

They were two-legged and two-armed, but they were huge and thickset and ungainly, their heads set right between their shoulders with little or no neck. Probably to compensate for this lack of head movement, they had eyes that stuck out on stalks like those of a snail. These stalks poked around in every direction, or they could be retracted right into the eye sockets. When that happened they just looked ordinarily ugly instead of horrible. Right away Valerie found herself thinking of the aliens as 'popeyes'.

Soon the square was crowded, and even though they were speaking their local language rather than Intergalactic Valerie could guess they were in holiday mood. The women — she supposed they were women — wore very bright shawls and fungus-like flowers in their fussy hats. There was a lot of shoving and pointing and laughing as they stared at the cages.

After a while Valerie just couldn't bear the sight of all the eyeballs rolling around on the end of their stalks, and she shut her own eyes and crouched on the bottom of her cage. A sudden sharp pain in her back made her jump and hit her head against the bars.

"Ow!" She looked round in time to see a small evil-looking popeye with a sharp stick. "Stop that, you beast," she yelled at him.

At once there was a surge of popeyes towards her cage, all of them reaching out to poke her to make her talk again. She was quite sore from all the prodding before she realized that as long as she yelled they were going to go on poking. After that she sat silently with her head down, not letting them see her anger or her tears, until they got bored and left her alone. She wished spitefully that the horrid little popeye would just try poking the wallaroon and get eaten for his cruelty. That'll teach it, she sniffed.

A bell rang and the crowd became relatively quiet. In the distance, out of sight, she could hear a single voice talking on and on. Speeches?

"Mr Ansnek, can you see what's happening?"

"It appears to be an auction." At that moment there was an excited cry and the stamping of feet on the pavement. "And the first lot has just been sold," he added.

"First lot of what?"

"Us. In the cages."

"Sold? But they can't do that. We're people. At least you and I are."

"My dear young person, I'm afraid that as far as these creatures are concerned you and I are animals just as much as the wallaroon, and our fates are likely to be similar. Sold as a pet, sent to the Zoo, or in my case—the laboratory bench."

Valerie wasn't even listening. "You can't sell people," she yelled at the popeyes, but they didn't seem to understand her Intergalactic, and they looked as if they didn't care anyway. Outlaws, Mr Ansnek had called them. Oh, what was she going to *do*?

Mr Ansnek was talking again. "Interesting coincidence," he said chattily, as if his fate didn't worry him a bit. "Two of the cages to my right contain creatures very similar to yourself."

She was worrying so much that it didn't sink in at first. Then... "*What* did you say?"

"I said that two of the cages contain beings somewhat similar to yourself. There goes one now up for auction. I imagine it will fetch a pretty penny. Nice-looking little thing."

Susan! Could Susan be here too? Without thinking, Valerie tried to stand up. She hit her head on the top of the cage and bit her tongue. "Susan!" she yelled as loudly as she could. "Are you there?"

"Val, is that you? Val, take me home. I'm scared. I want to go home."

"I can't, love. Not just now. But don't worry. I'll think of a way, I promise..." She couldn't help crying and through her sobs she could hear Susan wailing too. It was awful. Up until that moment she'd thought that being trapped alone on an alien planet was the worst thing that could possibly happen to her. But it wasn't. Knowing that Susan was here too, scared out of her wits, made it much worse. She's too young, she thought. Only five. She won't know how to fight back.

"It's wicked!" she yelled, but nobody was listening.

"Your sib?" Mr Ansnek asked sympathetically. "Don't worry. It's not going to the Zoo, I'll be bound. There, what did I say. See that enormous woman over there? She's the new owner. Cost a pretty penny, judging from the exclamations."

Valerie craned her neck past the bulk of the wallaroon and saw the huge popeye surge forward. She wanted to call out and ask her to be kind to Susan. To warn her that she caught cold easily and couldn't bear warm milk, and that she needed lots of sleep or she'd get cranky. Was the owner a kind person? You certainly couldn't tell from her expression, which was as wrinkled and peculiar as everyone else's.

With any luck Susan'll be warm and have enough to eat, Valerie tried to console herself, but the sight of her little sister being led through the crowd on a long red leash was too much for her and she burst into angry tears. "I'll find you," she yelled after Susan. "I'll get you away, I promise."

And I will too, she vowed to herself. If I have to spend the rest of my life finding a way, I will. She felt a pain, that was part of loving, shoot through her body, and when it had gone there was an awful empty feeling.

She tried to cheer herself up. If Frank saw Susan vanish he'll have told Mother and Father, and they'll have told the Federation Police. They'll find us in no time, she promised herself firmly. But her logical mind told her that if Susan had fallen into the space trap, Frank must have fallen too.

"Are you there?" she yelled as loudly as she could. "Frank!" But there was no answer and she told herself it was all right. Somehow he'd avoided the trap. Soon help would be on the way.

She became aware of a comparatively thin popeye standing in front of her cage. Thin by local standards, that is. He'd weigh well over a hundred kilograms back on Eden, she guessed. He walked all the way round her cage.

"Mr Ansnek, what's he doing?" she whispered, and the man took a small notebook from his pocket and began to scribble madly.

"I infer he is a scientist. He has been staring at me also and I feel he may have plans to dissect me. You too, I wonder?"

"Dissect?" Valerie's voice ran up the scale into a scream. The popeye winced and moved back but went on writing. "He's taking down our conversation. Everything we say. Do you suppose he understands Intergalactic? None of the others seemed to. Perhaps we could appeal to his better nature to let us go. Talk to him, Mr Ansnek, *please*."

But just then the popeye closed his notebook with a snap and tucked it into the pocket of his tunic, which was very drab compared with the holiday garb of the crowd and looked more like some kind of uniform. He turned and marched purposefully through the crowd, which fell back respectfully to give him room.

In a few minutes two popeyes, identically dressed in yellow coveralls, came to the front of Valerie's cage and unlocked the door. "What's happening? Where are they taking me? Mr Ansnek!"

As she was pulled from the cage she had a wild idea of just making a run for it there and then, out into the alien countryside beyond the houses and the cabbage trees, but she hadn't realized what a heavy planet this was. Her legs felt like lead, and to make things worse she had been cramped in the tiny cage. Before she had taken more than a single step her legs gave way and she fell forward onto all fours.

Pins and needles stabbed her calves. She tried to scramble to her feet again, telling herself that the pain would go off as soon as she started to walk. But the two attendants had a different idea. She was poked and prodded with metal rods that gave her a tingling shock with each prod, until she gave up. They forced her across the square on her hands and knees: just as if I really were an animal, she thought wretchedly.

Luckily she didn't have far to go. She was lifted into the high box-like back of a huge old-fashioned truck that had treads rather than wheels. The door was slammed and bolted. She heard the snick of a bar falling into place.

Someone climbed into the driver's seat and started the motor. There was a small diamond shaped window in the door, as well as some light coming from the heavy screen that separated the body of the truck from the driver's compartment. Valerie pressed her face against this window as the truck headed off down one of the yellow streets. She got a fast glimpse of a row of cages, but she didn't have time to guess which among them might hold Mr Ansnek. She would have liked to have said goodbye if there had been time. Now she was really alone.

The square was out of sight, and, since looking back was making Valerie feel a bit sick, she sat down on the floor close to the screen and tried to see where they were head-ing. They drove straight along a yellow road for a considerable distance. The houses thinned out and countryside took over. There was dry-looking turf and many more of the cabbage trees. In spite of her fear the motion lulled her into a doze, and she didn't know how much farther they had travelled before the truck turned abruptly to the right, pitching her forward. She jerked awake and blinked her eyes. They passed a set of splendid high-pillared gates and drove along what she guessed must be a private road. In the distance was a huge building with a sprawl of less important buildings scattered behind it.

The truck swerved away from the main block and drove round to the back and stopped suddenly. The driver climbed out. She could hear his footsteps crunching on the gravel. Then there was silence. She peered out of the back window but could see nothing but a set of closed doors.

The footsteps returned. There was a noise above her and suddenly the truck became brighter as a small door in the roof was opened. Something was tossed in, and before she could get to her feet the door was closed again. The inside of the truck seemed even darker than before.

What had the driver dropped in? Could it be food? It must be hours since she ate last, maybe even days. Her fingers groped along the floor until they found a cold hard cylinder as long as the palm of her hand. Nothing to eat anyway. She dropped it and sighed. Suddenly she became aware of a sickeningly sweet smell, so strong that she could taste it in her throat. Her tongue felt thick and her lips tingled and then went numb. Her eyes closed and she slid limply to the floor of the truck.

The Laboratory

Valerie woke with the muddled feeling that she had fallen asleep in Mother's lab back on Eden and had this weird dream. Through half-shut sleepy eyes she could see a white ceiling set with lighting panels, walls crowded with glass-doored cupboards, the metal cases of computerized testing equipment. Only something had gone wrong with her eyes. Why did everything look so huge?

She swung her legs down from the hard bench on which she'd been lying and sat up, blinking. No, this certainly wasn't Mother's lab, though it *was* a lab of some kind. "Mother?" she called. But the room was very quiet and completely empty.

She padded in her socked feet up and down aisles crowded with equipment. Everything seemed slightly wrong and out of sync. The table tops were too high, the handles of the upper cupboards completely out of reach, and the markings on the equipment were as strange as Sanskrit. She began to shiver and didn't want to look any more. She retreated to the bench she'd been sleeping on and curled up in a tight ball.

Go away, she told the room. You're not real. This isn't happening. It's a dream. But the bench was as hard under her side, the cover was as rough against her cheek, the alien bitter smell of the place was still in her nostrils. Oh, Mummy, I'm so scared. Slow tears leaked out from under her tightly closed eyelids.

There was a click and she heard a door open. She daren't move or open her eyes. If I don't move it'll go away, she thought hopefully. Heavy feet crossed the room and she could *feel* someone standing over her.

"Good morning, I am Dr Mushni," a voice said in halting Intergalactic, with such a heavy accent that she could hardly understand it. She didn't move even when she could feel him coming closer. "Ahah, excellent!" the thick voice went on.

She felt him move away and let out a little sigh of relief. Then he was back beside her and her eyes flew open in spite of themselves, for he was stroking her cheek with something cold and hard. She saw him insert a circular glass plate into one of the machines set on a high bench. After a moment's delay the machine began to chatter and then spat out a strip of pink paper like a long pale tongue.

"Very interesting! So you are from a watery planet? Not from the dry one where we found you."

"How do you know?" Valerie couldn't help asking the fat back of his head. It was bald and ruddy, rather like a tomato.

"The water from your eyes tells me something of the elements of your seas. Not that I am a chemist. I am a linguist. So, tell me, please, where you are from?"

He turned suddenly and came towards her, and she shrank back from him so quickly that she banged her head on the wall behind her. His face was deeply wrinkled and his ears were thick fleshy blobs with no real shape to them. His nose spread out across the middle of his face, with flaps that alternately opened and closed as he breathed. His lips, on the other hand, were thin and fleshless, no more than a slit in his face. His eyes, on the end of pink stalks, were of a mild blue, and waved continuously like a strange sea plant. They didn't look very fierce, only rather disgusting.

He stretched out a fat hand towards her and she shut her

eyes and swallowed. I won't scream and give him the satisfaction of knowing how scared I am, she told herself. No matter what he does, I just won't. She held her breath. But all that happened was that he rubbed the place on the back of her head that she'd banged on the wall. His hand felt warm and gentle. She was so surprised that she opened her eyes again.

"So tell me where you are from?" he asked.

"Delta Parvonis Three," she said, guessing that the name wouldn't mean anything to him. She made up her mind not to say a single word about Eden. The thought of these horrible popeyes setting up their traps on Eden, the centre of Galactic culture, just made her shiver.

"You must try to tell my astronomy friends exactly where that is," he said. "For myself, I know nothing about such matters. I am a linguist; that is to say, I study languages. I am very glad I heard you speak back in the market place. Otherwise you would have been sold or sent to the Zoo with the other animals. You see, I am making a study of alien thought processes. It is very difficult. Although we collect many interesting specimens in our traps, only once in a while do I find one who is able to communicate."

"Traps? How can you get away with it? How do you dare? You must know it's illegal."

The slit lips tightened and the eyes suddenly retracted into his head. He grew pale. "We are not part of the Federation, so why should we obey Federation laws? We go our own way and do as we choose, *alien*!"

Valerie said nothing, and after a moment the natural redness came back to Dr Mushni's face, and his eyes once more waved at the end of their stalks. "We have the most comprehensive collection of wild life in the Galaxy, I am sure. One day, if you are good, I shall take you to see it."

"Thank you." Valerie licked her lips. Her mouth felt

suddenly dry. "When I've helped you all I can and you've finished studying me, will you let me go back home?"

Dr Mushni began to shake so violently that his thick cheeks joggled up and down. His eyes vanished into their sockets and he made a horrible choking sound and turned even redder than usual. Valerie shrank back against the wall. I won't let him see how scared I am, she told herself, and forced herself to glare back at him, her lips tightly together so he couldn't see them trembling.

"Oh, ho, ho, that's very funny! Let you go home? Well, well..."

Angrily she realised that he was actually laughing at her.

"I don't think it's a bit funny," she snapped.

"You don't, eh? Well, tell me, on your own planet I expect they capture animals for zoos and experiments and things of that kind?"

"Ye...es," said Valerie cautiously.

"And when they are no longer useful they are taken back to the jungles or plains where they were found?"

"Of course not. That would be far too expensive..." She stopped and bit her lip.

"Exactly! Do you know how far it is to that desert planet where we found you? Well, neither do I, I'm no astronomer, but it could be anywhere up to six parsecs. And you want us to send you back!" He began to shake again.

"That's different. I'm a person. We don't do that to people back home, only to animals."

"And who is to decide what is an animal and what is a person? If I appeared on your home planet would you consider me a person? And who knows, perhaps a walla-roon is a person — to a wallaroon. It is very interesting to..."

Valerie was no longer listening. She had told Susan that she would get her back home. And I will, she promised herself. There must be a way. I'm just going to have to learn to be patient and please Dr Mushni and find out everything I possibly can about this place. But six parsecs! Thirty million million kilometres away from home. And I don't even know the direction, she thought despairingly. Then she gritted her teeth and looked squarely at Dr Mushni.

"So you chose me for your study of languages," she said as calmly as she could manage. "What can I do to help?"

"*Shnitzick!*" he exclaimed and rubbed his hands together. "Have you had enough sleep? I should like to begin at once."

"Could I have something to eat first? I haven't had a bite since breakfast on DeePeeThree and goodness knows how long ago that really is."

"What is 'breakfast'?"

"The first meal of the day."

"How many times do you eat? We feed most of the exotic animals twice a day, morning and night."

"Three times," said Valerie firmly.

"My goodness, a little scrap of a thing like you! What does 'breakfast' consist of?"

Valerie thought fondly of orange juice and honey crisps with cream and toast and wild smokeberry jam and tea. She sighed. "Some kind of fruit, perhaps. And whatever you make with grain. Bread? Cooked meal?"

"I'll see what I can do. Meanwhile you will find a bathroom through here." He opened a door off the lab to show her. The fixtures were so high that he had to find a box for Valerie to stand on to reach the basin.

When she came back to the lab, her face and hands washed and her hair smoothed back with her fingers, she felt a little better. There was a tray on one of the high work tables, laden with all sorts of strange food, some interesting looking, some quite repulsive.

"Try these. If they disagree with you we will have to have the vets make up some 'chow' to suit your metabolism, as they do for the zoo specimens."

Valerie hoped she would find something eatable. It was important to be able to survive on some of the native food, because if she were going to escape she would need to know exactly what was good and what made her sick, and where it grew. Dr Mushni is going to learn a lot from me, she thought, as she nibbled cautiously at the different foods. But that's nothing to what I'm going to learn from him!

Some of the food tasted horrible, but no worse than some of the things she disliked on Eden, like some extra smelly cheeses, or the *quintabble* fruit, which lots of people loved, but which to her tasted like something that had gone bad. I'll try everything and hope I don't get sick or come out in a rash.

She worried again about Susan and the kind of food she'd be getting. The problem was that at five she wasn't really old enough to know what was safe to try and what one should definitely say 'no' to. Maybe it would be possible to find out from Dr Mushni where she was and how she was being treated—without letting him suspect that she was her sister, or in any way interested in her. That was going to be difficult, but there were all sorts of possibilities. She began to feel more cheerful; maybe it was just not being so hungry any more.

Dr Mushni started work right away and kept at it for hours. He made her sit in a special chair with wires fastened to her head, facing a screen onto which he flashed pictures. They talked about what she saw and their conversation was recorded. But she got awfully tired sitting still for so long, and after a while her head ached and her eyes began to water from staring at the pictures. She wondered when he was going to stop.

I bet he doesn't have a wife or family, she thought. He probably lives in this lab and works until he drops and forgets to eat regularly, which is why he's thinner than most of the others.

"It is necessary for my health to have a walk before lunch," she told him firmly, when she couldn't bear to sit still for another minute. "And again before dinner if the weather is good." She held her breath, wondering if he would get angry or even hit her, but Dr Mushni stared at her with his mild blue eyes revolving.

"What an interesting idea. We will walk in the grounds of the Institute and converse. I have a pocket recorder, so no time will be wasted."

He rummaged in a drawer that seemed to be a catch-all for the kind of things that didn't really belong in a lab, like pieces of string and a broken knife for prising lids off things. Mother had one just like it at home, thought Valerie, with a pang of homesickness. After a search he brought out a collar, which he quickly snapped around Valerie's neck before she could protest. Then he clipped a chain onto the collar and shook it invitingly.

"Come then. We will walk."

Valerie followed him out of the lab and down a long undecorated corridor with closed doors on either side. She knew that she should pay lots of attention to where Dr Mushni was leading her, but she just couldn't, she was so mortified by the collar and chain. She kept her eyes down and when someone opened a door and stared at her she shrunk to the side of the corridor. To be on a chain!

The corridor turned to the right and opened onto a large area with pink and orange cubes scattered about, obviously for sitting on, and pots of plants with large fleshy leaves. She guessed it must be a reception area. There were a number of popeyes sitting around or talking in small groups.

Dr Mushni abruptly shortened the chain, so that Valerie choked and had to stay close to him, but it was too late. They had been seen. All the popeyes crowded around, patting and pinching, ruffling her hair and poking at her eyes to see why they would not pop out properly. She shrank against Dr Mushni's side, her hands to her face, while he shooed them away. I won't get angry or fight back, she told herself. If I did that they'd think I was dangerous and put me in a cage at the Zoo, and then I'll never get a chance to find Susan. I'll be the most obedient pet in the world, she vowed. Until they almost forget I'm here.

She followed Dr Mushni meekly when he jerked her chain and pulled her through the big front door away from the curious crowd. Once they were well away from the buildings he unclipped the chain and let Valerie go free. It was better then. The weather was mild, and the big orange balloon of the sun was comforting but not too hot. The short dry turf felt pleasant beneath her feet and even the disagreeable smell of the cabbage trees that dotted the grounds became unnoticeable after a while.

She worked even harder that afternoon, to show Dr Mushni how important fresh air and exercise were to her. By the time a tray arrived, laden with more alien food, she was tired out and her head was pounding. Some workmen had come and pulled the upper shelves from one of the many cupboards, leaving the lowest shelf to serve as a bed. It was not too uncomfortable with a pad of some stuff for a mattress and a couple of coarse blankets.

The tray was taken and the light switched off. Valerie heard the door shut with a click and she was alone. She ran to the door and listened. There was no sound. She turned the handle cautiously and pulled. It was locked, of course, but she had had to try.

She looked around. Almost no light came from the

window. It was too high for her to see out of and it was securely barred. The rest of the room was in darkest shadow, rows and rows of counters, shelves and cupboards, large and ominous.

She took a running jump across the room and back into bed and hid her head under the coarse blanket. It smelt, not of anything particularly bad, but just...alien. In the dark, lonely, odd-smelling night a strange wavering cry drifted in through the window. She shivered and began to cry.

The next day was a repetition of the first. She worked with Dr Mushni. They walked in the park of what he called 'The Institute'. They worked again until supper. And so every day. She didn't mind the hard work. When she was busy she didn't have time to think. What she dreaded were the long nights alone with her sad thoughts of Mother and Father and Frank and her worried thoughts about poor little Susan.

Funnily enough there were moments, especially running across the park meadow, when she forgot that she was a prisoner. Only they didn't last for long. Dr Mushni would blow his whistle and she had to go back to him and have the hateful chain clipped to her collar. But one day she ran across the grass and fell on her back, breathless, among some scrubby bushes. She stared up at the blue sky and felt a moment's peace. When Dr Mushni's whistle blew she couldn't bear to obey it. She ignored him, and then it became funny, as he ran to and fro, blowing the silly whistle and scolding her in a mixture of Intergalactic and Popeye.

He found her before too long and he didn't seem to think it was funny at all. He looked as if he were going to hit her, and she crouched down against the trunk of the bush. But all he did was snap the chain onto her collar and hold it so short and walk so fast that she had to run to keep up with him, her hands inside the collar to keep from choking. The next day he made her work right through the lunch hour and they never went outdoors at all. After that Valerie didn't play any more games and always obeyed the whistle.

The work went on and Valerie began to lose track of time, though she never for a single day stopped worrying about how she was going to get away and start looking for Susan. But how? And where? She hadn't dared rouse Dr Mushni's suspicion by talking about her. Then one day everything changed. Dr Mushni came into the lab with a frown on his wrinkled face. Valerie was quite accustomed to his ugliness by now, and could recognize his different moods by the way his eyes either twirled or retracted and by the widening or pouting of his mouth slit.

"What is the matter?"

"Nothing, Vally. Nothing. Let us get on with the work. We must do all we can by the end of this eight-day."

"Why?"

"Because my grant comes to an end then, and I am afraid the Institute doesn't find my project sufficiently interesting to continue it."

It took a moment for this to sink in. Her heart pounded painfully. "What becomes of *me*?"

Dr Mushni sighed. "It is *possible* that the Zoo might accept you, though you are not a very exciting specimen."

"If they don't..." For a moment hope glowed brightly. "If the Zoo doesn't want me, would you transmit me back to DeePeeThree? *Please*."

He hesitated. Then he said, "Yes, of course," and went on fastening the electrodes to her head.

She knew he was lying, and her stomach knotted with fear. By now he had taken her all over the Institute, and she knew where the experimental animals went to when they were no use any more, to a small room at the end of the lowest basement corridor. It had a door that slid across and a button on the outside. When the button was pressed the animal inside was turned back into the original atoms it was made of and a great deal of energy was released to help power the Institute. It was all very tidy and economical . . . and horrible.

She stared at Dr Mushni, hoping she had misunderstood his expression, but he turned his back on her and fussed with the apparatus. She felt cold all the way through. It was the longest day of her life. When it was over at last and she huddled under her rough blankets she still could not get warm. She shivered and thought about the basement corridor with the sliding door at the end of it.

If only Mum and Dad would come. Or Frank. She began to cry. But then she thought about Susan stuck with that awful fat woman for life — or until she got bored with her. What happens to pets here? she worried. Is there something like the Pets' Society for readoptions? Or were they tidily disposed of at the vet's or just dropped off in the country somewhere to fend for themselves?

"Susan's too young. She'll never manage. And I promised I'd get her away. I've *got* to go on living. I've *got* to find a way."

She stopped crying and sat up in bed and bit her nails and thought furiously until finally she came up with a plan. In the morning she was eagerly waiting when Dr Mushni came in with her breakfast.

"Dr Mushni, you are not happy that your grant is ending, are you? I have an idea. Would you like to hear it?"

"You? An idea?" He looked as surprised as if she were an elephant offering to vacuum the room with its trunk.

"The work is very interesting and you are so kind," she went on. Dr Mushni's pale eyes shot out and revolved with pleasure and confusion. "Your Intergalactic is perfect, but it is not a language that can tell you much about different peoples and how they think. It is a neutral language, intended for trade and commerce. If I were to teach you English and you were to teach me *your* language, think how much you would be able to find out about me and my people and the way we think. Far more than you could get from those brain scans."

Dr Mushni clapped his stubby hands together. "*Schnitznik*! What a magnificent idea. You will cooperate with me? For a project like this I know I will get a grant. I will write a book. I will become famous. I may even get a pension and live out my life in honoured retirement with students listening to my words..." He stared out of the window in a dream of future glory.

Then he came out of the dream, clapped his hands together again and bustled over to his desk. "No work today, Vally. I shall be too busy writing the proposal." Sitting meekly on her bed while Dr Mushni scribbled and tore up and scribbled again, Valerie thought the day would never end. But it's worth it, she encouraged herself. If only they'll accept the proposal. He seems so sure. But... She began to bite her fingernails again.

Within an eight-day, Dr Mushni had the news that his proposal had been accepted. Practically unlimited funds would be at his disposal, he told her gleefully. "Anything I want. You must tell me if you can think of anything that would be useful."

"Goodness, you don't need any more machinery. Just a portable voice recorder. You see, the important thing for us to do is to develop a really broad vocabulary, and we can only do that by travelling around the country and seeing as much as possible."

He frowned at that. "It will not be easy, Vally. The sight of a creature as ugly as yourself could cause a riot. You have only been exposed to the scientific community up until now. I will have to be very careful, for your sake as well as the project's."

It was infuriating to be called ugly by a creature with a huge wrinkled bald head, nose flaps, thick ears, a slit mouth and eyes on stalks; but Valerie swallowed her pride and looked as meek as she could.

"I'm sure you'll be able to think of plenty of safe places until we see how it goes," she soothed him. And of course he did.

They took some very dull drives through the streets of the nearby city, in a closed car with shaded windows. They toured a number of factories where incomprehensible things were made, all of them squat and ugly to Valerie's eyes, and in the favourite popeye colours of pink, orange and purple. But it was hard to tell Dr Mushni the English word for something she didn't understand herself, like that oval with legs all round and a shallow depression at one side. Was it a statue? Or something as ordinary as an end table or a barbecue? She asked Dr Mushni to take her somewhere else where they could look at things they could really talk about.

So Dr Mushni took her to the Zoo. It was about twenty minutes drive from the Institute and seemed to be a very important place indeed. In fact, though she wasn't sure of this, it seemed that the Institute was a small part of the Zoo. Or was it the other way round?

They had a very interesting time and there was plenty to talk about. The wallaroon was there, as morose as ever, in a specially designed habitat that was supposed to be like its own planet. Dr Mushni and Valerie had a long talk about primates, while it stared at them from beneath the heavy black dome of its forehead.

Seeing the great man-eating ape again reminded Valerie of Mr Ansnek. She felt guilty at having forgotten about him. Was he somewhere in this vast Zoo, she wondered hopefully, in spite of his fears of dissection?

Their conversation was so successful that Dr Mushni told Valerie that they would be coming back for several days, until indeed they had exhausted all the possibilities of the Zoo. He hurried her back to the lab so that he could process the talk tapes through the computer. He was almost breathless with excitement.

Valerie was breathless too. Even though she was getting stronger the planet's gravitational pull still made her feel that she had suddenly gained twenty kilograms. And how can I run away when I feel so heavy? she thought despairingly. But then she cheered herself up. I'm thin and I can still move and think faster than the popeyes. I must exercise secretly and keep in shape. Just in case.

The next day at the Zoo she kept an eye out for Mr Ansnek, but he was in none of the cages or habitats they explored. It would have helped if she had known what he looked like. All she had to go by was a dry educated voice and a kind manner.

They passed a Zoo parking lot and she saw several cars and trucks with the same symbol that she'd seen on the thornbush trunk back in the maze on DeePeeThree. Millions and millions of kilometres away. She shivered at the thought. How had the popeyes got to DeePeeThree in the first place? She hadn't seen a single aeroplane, and if they hadn't developed flight how could they have got out into the Galaxy? Yet the Zoo was crowded with exotic specimens. It was a puzzle...

"Vally!" Dr Mushni was talking to her. She pulled herself together and paid attention.

"Today I want to show you another primate, a very strange creature. It is like you in some respects — the same hairy head and sunken eyes, the same grossly smooth face. You will be able to name for me in English all the parts of its body and tell me how and why they differ from yours." Dr Mushni was very excited.

He hustled her along one of the brick walks and around a corner to where a large cage stood. "It is not in a habitat yet, as the scientists here are puzzled by its behaviour patterns and are not sure what is an appropriate background for it."

By now Valerie too was curious to see this unusual specimen. She could see that the cage was large and clean with a supply of fresh straw scattered over the floor, except in one corner where a makeshift hut stood, constructed of pieces of wood, sacking and sheets of plastic.

"It built that itself," Dr Mushni told Valerie. "Like a huge nest. Fascinating, isn't it? Too bad we do not have a pair."

There was nothing to see yet, but a sign on the front of the cage said, 'Feeding Time 21:00'. Valerie was getting quite good at reading Popeye, though her tongue could never properly manage the grunts and squeals and sneezes that went into the spoken language.

A crowd began to gather in the open square in front of the new cage. Dr Mushni kept Valerie in a shady place at the back, where she would not be so noticeable. At length a keeper appeared, dressed in the yellow coveralls worn by all the Zoo and Institute staff, and unlocked the door.

The crowd drew back with little cries of "Careful there!" And "*Schnitznik*! I wouldn't go in there for a hundred *skrallia*."

There was a trough close to the front of the cage and into it the keeper poured a bucketful of mash. Then he nipped smartly through the door and had it locked behind him before the smell of food had penetrated to the occupant of the makeshift den.

Everyone in the crowd waited, eyes extended to their maximum length, so that from above the square must have looked like a sea of gently moving eyeballs.

"Ah!" Someone near the front pointed. A stir went through the crowd. The eyeballs lined up in the same direction. Something was moving in the ramshackle shelter.

Then an incredibly thin figure, almost a skeleton, emerged from the den and stood upright. It had a pale face, with matted hair hanging from head and chin. It blinked in a dazed way and then teetered on its matchstick legs over to the trough. There it squatted, scooped the slop in its front paw and ladled it into a fleshy hole in the front of its hairy face. The crowd cheered and laughed and pressed closer to the bars, staring at the creature.

It crouched silently over the trough, scooping up the food and sucking it eagerly off palms and fingers. It never raised its sunken eyes to the crowd, and Valerie heard a comment that perhaps this strange creature didn't have proper eyes at all. As soon as the trough was empty, the creature turned its back on the crowd and shambled back to its den. Everyone sighed regretfully and moved on to the next exhibit.

Dr Mushni chattered excitedly. "Amazingly deviant, isn't it? I wonder that it can balance on legs like that. It *is* similar to you in some ways, do you not think, Vally? I hope you are not insulted by my saying this. I speak as a scientist. You are much less ugly. You are not so tall or thin, nor are you as hairy. But there are similarities, do you not think? Vally, are you listening...?"

Valerie was still staring at the pathetic pile in the corner that the creature had built. Her face was white and drawn, and she hadn't heard Dr Mushni at all. For one topsy-turvy moment she had seen the alien primate with the same eyes as the crowd. It was crazy, but after all she hadn't seen a single human being since she'd been snatched from the maze on DeePeeThree. But not to recognize her very own brother, Frank!

Mr Isnek Ansnek

Valerie felt as if the ground had dropped out from under her. Frank was a prisoner here, too, and there was no one on DeePeeThree to tell Mother and Father about the trap in the thorn bush. If it wasn't discovered the Federation Police would never find them, never. The Galaxy was just too huge.

Poor Frank! So thin and dirty and ill-looking. She shut her eyes and took a deep breath, forcing herself to stand still, not to run across the square to the cage and call to him, tell him she was here. The ground rocked under her feet and she grabbed the nearest solid object, which happened to be Dr Mushni's arm.

"What is it? Are you ill?"

With an enormous effort she pushed the picture of her dirty half-starved brother out of her mind, and the even worse picture of all of them trapped on this awful planet for ever and ever. She let go his arm and opened her eyes. She took another deep breath and actually managed a small tight smile.

"Ill? Goodness, no. It's just..." She thought quickly. "Well, the crowd was so very big. I haven't seen so many of you all at once before."

Dr Mushni nodded understandingly. "I am sure that if I were surrounded by a crowd of beings like yourself I too would be upset, even nauseated. You are sure you are well?

All right. I was asking you about the similarities between yourself and that specimen."

"I noticed more differences than similarities," Valerie said quickly. Was it too quickly? Dr Mushni gave her a surprised look and she forced a laugh. "I certainly hope I'm not as ugly as that specimen."

Her answer seemed to satisfy Dr Mushni and he turned and led her along the brightly coloured paths, away from the crowds, to continue their talk.

I must never let him suspect Frank's my brother, thought Valerie, as she followed obediently on the leash. Because if he knew, he'd watch me twice as closely and never give me the chance of talking to him. And I must. I simply must. If we can just get together we'll think of a plan.

So when Dr Mushni said, "It would be interesting to compare blood and saliva types and see how closely you are related to those specimens," she didn't even jump.

"Yes, it would," she agreed. She was amazed at how calm her voice could be with the turmoil that was going on inside her. Thank goodness she was Type A and Frank was O. That might put them off the scent a bit. "Did you notice, he even has five fingers as I do? I suppose, if you were to go far enough back in Galactic history, you might find that our ancestors both came from Earth, maybe a thousand years ago."

She managed to go on talking lightly in this way, and taught Dr Mushni several language concepts that were new to him, but every minute was torture and it seemed an age before he was ready to walk back to the main gate and drive her back to the Institute.

When at last she was alone, after Dr Mushni had removed her supper tray and locked her in the laboratory for the night, she sat down on her bed with a sob and rubbed her hands over her face. It felt quite stiff and sore with all the smiling she'd been doing.

Why was Frank so dazed and ill-looking? Why hadn't he answered her shout in the market the way Susan had done? It was that silence that had given her the hope that somehow he had escaped the trap and was safely on DeePeeThree with Mother and Father. And how was she ever going to escape Dr Mushni's constant presence and talk to him?

These thoughts went churning round and round in her head until she pulled herself together. Stop being so stupid, she told herself firmly. Stop worrying about the past. Concentrate on planning an escape from the Institute. Then you can go to the Zoo and talk to Frank. If you can't get away from Dr Mushni during the day you must go at night, when the Zoo is deserted and everyone asleep. Except for guards. There were bound to be guards. They were the first problem.

The second problem was how to actually *get* to the Zoo. It would be a very long walk. Out of the front gate of the Institute, a right turn, and then another right. About ten minutes driving, and a third right turn along a yellow road, and there was the main entrance. Could she do it without being seen? She couldn't move fast on this heavy planet.

Three right turns. Why, she'd be practically back where she started! She suddenly remembered her first night at the Institute, alone in the lab, and the strange yawning cry that had scared her. Later, Dr Mushni had explained. "Oh, it is just from the Zoo. You will soon get used to it. We all do."

Three right turns. Just because the road to the Zoo took twenty minutes by car didn't mean that there wasn't a quicker way. If there wasn't any path she would scramble through the scrub, over a couple of back walls, and with any sort of luck she'd be in the grounds of the Zoo.

Suddenly it all began to seem possible. She jumped off her bed and began to walk up and down the passageways between the high work benches that divided the laboratory. One thing she had noticed was that Zoo personnel wore the same kind of yellow coveralls as the Institute staff. It shouldn't be a problem to find a set that more or less fitted her. She'd seen some stuffed into one of the cupboards that lined the walls of the lab. Then all she'd have to do would be to get out of the lab and find an open side door to sneak out of.

That was all! She sighed and threw herself down on her bed again. How in Eden was she ever going to unlock the lab door and even begin to carry out the rest of her plan? The locks were not the old-fashioned kind that opened with a key, which, she imagined vaguely, could be picked with a screwdriver or a length of wire or something. These locks were up-to-date electronic jobs, opened with a magnetic card. Dr Mushni kept *his* card in the front pocket of his uniform tunic, and she had never seen him put it down anywhere, not even for a minute.

The outside doors would work on the same principle. During the day the front one was open, but then the foyer was always crowded and there were guards. And anyway she was on a leash during the day. At night there would be no guards, but how could she get out?

Forget it and go to sleep, she told herself. She lay down and shut her eyes tightly. At once she saw the sad collection of sticks and sacks and straw that was Frank's only home. She kept seeing his filthy face and the lack of any sort of hope in his slumped shoulders and shambling walk.

Oh, bother, this is hopeless! How can I possibly sleep? She got up again and began to prowl around the lab, looking in the doors and cupboards that lined the walls and the underside of the work benches. There must have been hundreds of them, small and big, all filled with neat rows of apparatus that had no meaning at all for her. If there *were* something there, useful for picking an electronic lock, she wouldn't recognize it anyway.

Tired tears began to run down her cheeks, and though she wiped them away angrily, they kept flowing. We're all prisoners, she thought hopelessly, and we'll be prisoners until we die. If I don't know where I am, how could Mother and Father? Or the Federation Police? And the Galaxy is so very big... She went back to bed at last and finally fell asleep.

Then it was morning and the warm orange light of the sun was coming in through the high lab windows. After a night's sleep hope had returned, and with it courage. I won't give up. Not ever! I'll go through every drawer and cupboard in the lab. It doesn't matter that I don't know what I'm looking for. I must just look. When I see something useful I'll know.

It was hard to get through the day, pretending everything was normal, talking to Dr Mushni and his voice-recorders all the long morning and the longer afternoon.

As soon as she was safely locked in the lab after supper she began her search, starting, for want of a better place, at the long wall that faced the window and the closet in which was her bed. The entire wall was lined with glass-fronted cupboards from counter to ceiling. Below the counters were alternate sections of drawers and big cupboards.

By the time she had searched the whole of the first wall she felt like giving up. But she went on looking, opening and shutting each drawer and cupboard, scrambling up on a high stool to look in the upper ones. Perhaps Dr Mushni kept a duplicate card in one of the drawers. Wouldn't that be marvellous? She allowed herself to hope and went on looking.

She came to the very end of the long wall and had begun to search the cupboards under the first row of counters when she heard a slight noise just outside the door. She banged an open cupboard door shut, switched off the light and leapt for her bed.

When Dr Mushni entered she was lying curled up under her blanket. Her heart was pounding like mad, but she forced herself to breathe quietly and evenly. It was all right. Dr Mushni paid no attention to her at all. She could hear his shoes clumping down the length of the lab. There was the rattle of an opening drawer. A silence that seemed to go on for ever, in which her pounding heart was the loudest noise in the room. Then an exclamation of pleasure, as if he'd found what he'd been looking for.

The drawer was closed. His feet clumped heavily back to the door. The light went out and the door clicked shut. She let out her breath in a long thankful sigh, but for a while she daren't move again. This time she'd been lucky. But suppose Dr Mushni *had* caught her snooping? In a peculiar way they had become almost friends, but if he no longer trusted her then life would become unbearable. He might send her away to the Zoo or to that last basement room. She lay under her blanket, weighing up the odds against him interrupting her again.

She made herself wait a full half-hour, counting off the seconds and minutes, and even after she had turned on the light she stood close to the door and listened with straining ears; but there was nothing to hear but a faint hum from one of the lights and a distant yawning cry from the Zoo. She took a deep breath and tiptoed back to the place where she had stopped searching.

Then she stopped suddenly. Her heart thumped. One of the lower cupboard doors had swung open. If Dr Mushni had seen that! Thank goodness he had walked up another aisle. She shut it firmly and at once the one next to it burst open. Behind the two doors was one very long cupboard. When you shut one door suddenly the air inside the cupboard forced open the other one, unless you were careful and not in a hurry. So that's how it had happened!

Within the cupboard was an exceedingly long box, and

she squatted down to look at its contents. They were bits and pieces of metal, finished in a dull black paint. The shapes were oddly familiar and the proportions seemed 'right' to her for the first time on this planet, where everything was always overlarge and clumsy. She pulled out a long curved tube, with wires protruding from one end. The other end split unexpectedly into five neat segments. She stared at them. Four fingers and a thumb.

"URGH!" Valerie dropped it on the floor. There was an awful clatter in the silence of the night, and Valerie stood poised ready for flight. But it was all right. Nobody had heard. She picked up the metal arm and laid it back in the long box with what she now recognized as another arm, a torso and two long thin legs. A robot! How silly of her. But what an odd place to keep a dismantled robot, she thought idly, closing the door and opening the one next to it.

She bent down to look into the next cupboard. Two yellow eyes stared intelligently back into hers. Valerie screamed and slammed the door shut and leaned against it. She was trembling. The door next to it swung slowly open.

"No!" she moaned and shut the second door. She was sweating, though the lab wasn't that warm, and she could feel the hair on the back of her head and neck prickle with fear.

"Pray do not shut me in again." A small dry voice spoke from within the cupboard. It was precise, though muffled. "I have barely enough energy left to talk."

Valerie swallowed. "Who . . . what are you?"

"We have already introduced ourselves." The voice was quietly reproachful. "My name is Isnek Ansnek."

"Oh, Mr Ansnek, I'm so glad to see you!" Valerie dropped to her knees and opened the door wide. "At least . . ." She looked at the long box with the various parts of Isnek Ansnek neatly laid in it and the head balanced on its neck on the shelf beside it. "Oh, dear," she finished weakly.

"My sentiments entirely. I am most thankful that you have at last come to my aid. Powerful though my intellect is, I had been quite unable to think of a practical way of reassembling my own body."

"How do you manage to talk?" Valerie asked curiously and then blushed. "I'm sorry. That was rude. It's just I'm not used to... well... talking to someone like you."

"I will overlook the rudeness. In any case an enquiring mind is a most desirable feature in the young. You must realize that I have no need of lungs or diaphragm or even vocal chords. My speaking voice is produced from within my head... What is wrong with you now?" he added severely.

Valerie found herself half laughing, half crying. She choked and took a deep breath. "I'm sorry. It's a bit of a shock, sitting here talking to you like this. You see, I quite thought you were dead. I didn't know you were a robot, you see."

"I might as well have been dead, shut up in a dark cupboard with no energy source to sustain me. It's most fortunate you left the door open just then. Though careless," he added severely. "The enemy might well have observed it."

"I didn't mean to..." Valerie began, and then stopped herself. This is silly, she thought. I don't have to apologize to a *robot*. "Is there anything I can do for you, Mr Ansnek?" she went on politely.

"Yes, indeed there is. I'll thank you to reassemble me."

"But I can't do that. I don't know the least thing about... I haven't any tools... suppose I put you together wrong?"

"I will be your guide, of course. There's nothing to it. As the ancient song says: 'The thigh bone's connected to the hip bone.'" Mr Ansnek's mouth opened and a strange raspy sound came from it. After a minute Valerie realised that he was actually laughing, as well as he could without a chest to act as a resonator.

"Well..." she said doubtfully. "All right then. Where do I begin?"

"Clear the counter above me and lay me out. Head first please. I'm still not getting all that much power down here."

So with two reverent and rather sweaty hands, Valerie lifted Mr Ansnek's head and placed it upright on the counter. Then she lifted out the torso, which was surprisingly heavy, almost more than she could handle.

"Don't drop me now. Careful. Easy there." Mr Ansnek's eyes rolled as he watched her progress. "Now my arms and legs. I hope they're somewhere around here. I won't be much use without them."

"It's all right," Valerie said cheerfully. "They're in the box too." She lifted his limbs out one by one and laid them on the counter at each corner of Mr Ansnek's torso.

"That won't do at all," snapped Mr Ansnek. "You're a big girl, for goodness' sake. Can't you even tell a right leg from a left one?"

"Sorry." Valerie blushed and switched the legs. "Now what do I do?"

"We will start with the legs and work up," he went on bossily. She didn't really mind his moods. After all, being all in pieces must be very upsetting. "Put my head on my stomach so I can see what's going on. Right. Now you're going to have to make two different kinds of connections there, mechanical ones and electrical ones. You'll need a set of screw-drivers, needle-nosed pliers, a soldering iron and some gold solder."

It's lucky Dr Mushni's so neat, thought Valerie, going to the bank of drawers that had in it every possible kind of tool. "But I don't know about gold solder," she said aloud after a search, standing on tiptoe to see into the higher drawers.

"I'll be a mess without it. Keep looking, there's a good girl."

But the best that Valerie could come up with was a heavy roll of solder that Mr Ansnek peered at and pronounced to be silver. "Perhaps this planet is as deficient in the heavier metals as it is in morals. It will have to do. So let's begin, there's a good girl."

Slowly, fumbling and butter-fingered at first, and with many scoldings from Mr Ansnek, Valerie began to put him back together. The false dawn of the white sun was paling the sky outside the lab by the time Valerie had got to the head. It was much worse than the rest. Not only was it very complicated indeed, with dozens and dozens of connections, but Mr Ansnek was no longer able to supervise the work from his former position on top of his torso. They managed with a metal dish instead of a mirror, many descriptions from Mr Ansnek and many false starts from Valerie.

She made a careful connection and soldered it neatly. She was quite proud of her soldering, and she had only burned her hand once. Mr Ansnek's right knee gave a terrific jerk, and she dropped the soldering iron. "Oh, dear, I'm so sorry. Did that hurt?"

"Try not to be so silly," said Mr Ansnek crossly. "And do get on with it. I've got pins and needles in that leg now. I hope you haven't broken the soldering iron. Even if there should be another one, it'll take some explaining to the enemy."

Valerie went on working silently, her tongue between her teeth. She wished that he didn't have to be quite so bossy, really every bit as bad as Frank used to be. And it bothered her when he called Dr Mushni 'the enemy'.

Of course he *was* in a way, she told herself. But he was a funny old thing, and he'd really been very kind to her. Of course, being dismantled and left in a dark cupboard might have prejudiced Mr Ansnek's feelings.

By the time he had been put together to his satisfaction and some minor adjustments made, the orange blush of the big sun was colouring the patch of sky outside the windows. Valerie stood back and looked proudly at her handiwork. It was the very first time that she had ever assembled a whole robot.

Mr Ansnek slid cautiously down from the counter and walked up and down the lab. "Well, all I can say is I hope I don't have to be out in the rain much. I can't wait to get back to civilization and put in for a refit."

As thanks went it could have been more gracious, but Valerie was past caring. She yawned until her jaw cracked. "You'll have to hide in that cupboard during the day," she reminded him. "And we'll just have to hope that Dr Mushni doesn't go looking for something in there."

He climbed in, grumbling quietly, and Valerie closed the doors very carefully. "I'll see you tonight," she told him, and then quickly tidied everything away and fell thankfully into bed.

Her last thought, before sliding down into a dark dreamless sleep, was that at least she wasn't alone any more. She had a friend.

5

The Escape

Thinking about Isnek Ansnek got Valerie through the next day, which began badly by her sleeping in so heavily that Dr Mushni had to shake her hard to get her to wake up at all. Then the sight of his eyes rolling anxiously at the end of their pink stalks made her scream.

"You are sick, Vally?"

"No, no. I'm sorry. Honestly I'm fine." Valerie scrambled out of bed to show just how fine she was. She swayed and yawned. How much sleep had she had? It felt like ten minutes. "I was dreaming that I was at home," she improvised. "And you surprised me, that's all."

"You're sure? I could ask one of the Zoo vets to check you over."

"I'm perfectly well," Valerie promised, and had to make up for the bad beginning by being extra bright, extra cheerful, extra helpful. By suppertime she had a pounding headache. She ate the thick soup that was provided and wrapped the dry stuff in a towel and hid it in her bed. Frank would be glad of food that wasn't slops once he'd got away, she thought. Oh, how wonderful it was going to be to see him again. She couldn't wait...

When she was alone at last she ran across the lab and opened Isnek Ansnek's cupboard. "Are you awake?" she whispered.

"Stupid question. I never sleep." The robot climbed stiffly

out of the cupboard and stretched himself. "Ah, good to feel the light again. Well, shall we leave?"

Valerie stared. "But where do you intend to go? And how? Shouldn't we make a plan first? There's Frank to rescue and Susan..."

"I intend to find the matter transmitter that brought me here, reverse the field and get off this objectionable planet."

"Where to? How'll you know how to use it, even if you can find this whatever-you-called-it...transmitter?"

"I'm sure my intellect is up to it. As to where, frankly I don't care. I can think of few places more disagreeable than this, except for planets that are a hundred per cent water...or sulphuric acid," he added thoughtfully. "Are you coming?"

"But I can't just go off like that. First of all there's Frank to rescue from the Zoo. Then we've got to find Susan, and I have no idea at all where she is. And it's all very well for you, but I've *got* to go home, or at least to an oxygen planet with the right pressure and so on."

"Pity." Mr Ansnek moved to the window.

"What are you doing now?"

"I'm just about to melt the frame and lift out the bars and the glass. Don't be alarmed. It won't be noisy. Nobody will come, nor will they know how I have left."

"You're going without me? But you're my *friend*. I put you together, didn't I? You've got to help me get Frank out of the Zoo. You can't just go off like that." Valerie burst into tears.

"My dear girl, please don't *cry* over me. Salt tears too, horribly corrosive." He shuddered. "As to your very mixed up statements: friendship is meaningless; you did assemble me; I don't have to help you with Frank, whatever a 'Frank' is; and of course I can go off. Why should I not?"

"Because ... oh, how can I possibly explain, if you don't even believe in friendship." Valerie wrung her hands. "You must understand kindness. You were kind to me in the market place. You warned me about the wallaroon."

"How very odd." Isnek Ansnek turned from his inspection of the window frame to stare at her. "Are you trying to tell me that because I saved you from being mauled by that overgrown ape I put myself under some future obligation to you? What a curious idea."

"No, of course I didn't mean that. I was just ... just appealing to your better nature. That's it."

"Hmmm." Isnek Ansnek stood with his black head tilted to one side, as if listening to some inner voice. "My better nature tells me that to preserve myself is the ultimate good," he said at last.

"Don't you have some directive about putting the safety of humans before your own needs?" Valerie asked despairingly.

"Oh, the old Asimov rules for robots." Isnek laughed lightly. "My goodness, that was all a very long time ago, wasn't it? I'm happy to say that, on Ilenius at least, we robots have had our freedom for many centuries. So, goodbye, my dear. Thank you for reassembling me. Not a bad job for a beginner, not bad at all. No hard feelings, I hope?" He held out a cold metal hand and Valerie found herself shaking it.

She sniffed and wiped her eyes with her sleeve. "Well, I may as well escape with you," she said bravely. "I'm not going to stay here and have Dr Mushni find out you're missing. He'll be bound to blame me for it and I'll finish up in the Zoo with Frank. Or more likely in the Basement Room," she added with a shiver.

"What basement room is that, and why are you suddenly so pale?"

Valerie explained. The robot was silent for a time. Then

he made a noise of disgust. "Tchah, humanoids! Why, we robots treat each other better than that." He was silent again. "Where will you go?"

"To the Zoo. At least I'll have the chance to talk to Frank. He's bound to have all sorts of good ideas. Maybe I'll be able to unlock his cage. Then we'll just make for the hills."

"Do you have the keys?"

"No, of course not. But at least I'm going to *try* to get him out," she shouted, goaded into forgetting caution.

"Ssssh! Not so loud." Isnek Ansnek sighed and sat down on one of the high lab stools. "Perhaps you had better explain to me about Frank and Susan and why they are more important than your own safety."

She told him, going back to the beginning, with school on Eden and the summer holidays on DeePeeThree. She told him about the maze with the trap at its centre and about waking up on the way to the market. "And this horrible fat creature went off with Susan, and who knows if she's treating her properly? Too many sweets and not enough exercise, I should think, judging by the way *she* looked. Or maybe she'll get bored with her and drown her like a puppy or drop her out of a car somewhere in the country. And I can't bear it, because it's all my fault, because I got grouchy and wouldn't babysit. And there's poor Frank, filthy dirty and looking as if he didn't care any more, not a bit like Frank. If you knew him you'd understand. I mean, he's super-intelligent and good-looking and nice too. Well, almost always."

Isnek Ansnek edged away as tears started to pour down Valerie's face. "My goodness," he said, but quite kindly. "What an illogical young person you are. Perhaps you were a trifle disagreeable to your family. But to blame yourself for the Space Trap is ridiculous. Sooner or later someone would have walked into it. Would you rather it had been your father or mother?"

"Of course not."

"Well then, you silly little girl, stop crying. I am sure I shall regret it, as it is a most illogical decision, but I will stay long enough to help you find your brother and sister and get them away. Not a moment longer, mind," he added severely.

"Of course not. Oh, Mr Ansnek, *thank* you."

"Now what you need is a good night's sleep. I don't want you twitching and jumping and crying when we break into the Zoo, now do I?"

"But..."

"Your brother can wait one more day. And I suppose I can too. Back to that boring cupboard." He sighed. "Luckily my mental resources are unlimited." He climbed in and lay down. "How do I look?"

"Pretty good. Mr Ansnek, thank you."

"You already said that. Don't mention it. Remember to shut the door, child. Goodnight."

Mr Ansnek was right. A night's sleep made all the difference. She wasn't depressed or weepy the next day. But it was a dreadful day all the same and seemed to go on for ever. Perhaps it was the feeling that tonight she would be free that made her captive life, in spite of Dr Mushni's kindness, fret against her soul like rough cloth against chapped skin.

Because she felt so different inside she was terrified that Dr Mushni would realise that something was wrong. Once or twice she thought he glanced at her sharply, extending his eyes and waving them rapidly from side to side. But perhaps she was mistaken. After all, his expression *was* alien to her. Even the robot's face held more humanity.

Suppertime came, and she cleaned everything off her tray, again wrapping all the solid food in a cloth. Then she lay impatiently, staring at the square of window from which the red light of the big sun slowly faded. Oh, hurry up. Let it be dark.

Shadows crept across the huge laboratory. She listened for a long time to the silence before sitting up and swinging her legs down from her bed. At that exact moment there were footsteps, the heavy thudding footsteps that still gave her the shivers, they were so unhuman. And there were voices, twittering together in Popeye. She lay down again and smoothed out her blanket, her heart thumping. That had been close!

The door swung open and for an instant the oblong of light lit two figures in the doorway. Then the switch was touched and the room flooded with light.

Valerie sat up. It wasn't hard to act bewildered, as if she had just been awakened. She shaded her eyes. "What...what is it?"

"Vally, come here." Dr Mushni's voice was much more domineering than usual, and she wondered if it had anything to do with his companion. She scrambled to her feet and walked quickly across the lab to where he stood by the open door. "Honoured sir, this is the specimen I told you about." Dr Mushni bowed deeply.

Valerie looked up cautiously. The second popeye was much larger than Dr Mushni, almost a giant in a place where two metres height was the norm. His face was deeply seamed and puckered. His expression was unreadable, but as she looked up at him she felt deeply afraid. Why was he here? And why now of all times? She lowered her eyes and looked meekly at the enormous feet of the stranger.

"Not a very intelligent-looking specimen. Couldn't you have found someone better to work with?" He spoke in Popeye, but Valerie understood and flushed angrily. He chuckled, not a pleasant sound. "I want to run some tests."

"Yes, sir." Dr Mushni bowed as deeply as his stomach would allow him. "When would be convenient?"

"No time like the present."

"Now?" Dr Mushni's eyes rotated rapidly. As for Valerie, she could feel herself turning white and hoped that she wasn't going to faint or do anything else stupid that might make this awful popeye feel she was not worth keeping. Oh, if only Mr Ansnek and she had escaped the previous night. If only... She managed to stay upright, her eyes on the floor, her nails digging into the palms of her hands.

"Yes, now!" The strange popeye snorted. "I have to give a paper to a very important group the day after tomorrow. I want to see if this new specimen of yours has anything useful to add. It would be a great thing for the Institute if we could justify the expense of the..." He used a word in Popeye which Valerie had never heard before. "And increase our standing at the expense of the Zoo, eh?"

Valerie realized that the popeye was talking just like some of her father's colleagues, the ones who annoyed him because they'd do almost anything to make a point and get money for their particular project. Father wasn't like that. "Which is why we'll never be rich," Mother had said, but laughing. Valerie knew she was on Father's side.

Understanding this made her feel better, though she was still somewhat afraid of the giant. He turned abruptly and went out, jerking his head to indicate that Dr Mushni and Valerie were to follow.

They walked along the corridor towards the main entrance. Valerie had a crazy impulse to make a dash for it when she saw the glass doors so close and darkness creeping up around the buildings outside. But, almost as if he read her mind, Dr Mushni's hand tightened on her wrist, and she was whisked down a further corridor and into a laboratory that was crowded with electronic equipment.

Two popeyes stood up as the door swung open and the giant strode in. They leapt forward, and before Valerie had time to protest, they had fastened her in a huge chair, with straps around her legs, arms and head. She began to feel deeply afraid.

Were they going to torture her? Make her tell about Frank and about Mr Ansnek and their plans to escape. But that's ridiculous, she told herself firmly. They can't know anything, and I won't tell them. Whatever it is they're after I must remember that I'm as sharp as they are. So when the technicians covered her head with a cap that was wired to a console beside the chair where she lay, she made her mind as blank as she possibly could, and very deliberately recited to herself every piece of poetry that she had ever learned. When she had finished that she went onto the multiplication table and the lists of irregular verbs in English and Intergalactic. Then she ran out of ideas and said 'the cat sat on the mat' over and over.

If the giant popeye had thought to ask her any questions things might have turned out very differently, but he was the kind of scientist who believed his machines were the best way of explaining the world around him. It was evident that he despised Dr Mushni for wasting his time talking to Valerie, almost as if they were equals, instead of sucking information out of her brain with his scanning machine.

In the middle of the hundred and fifty-first cat-sat-on-the-mat the cap was taken off Valerie's head. She was unstrapped and allowed to sit up. The giant was looking in a baffled way at the reams of pink paper that the machine had spewed onto the laboratory floor. "Very interesting," he said slowly. "Dr Mushni, I would like to consult with you further, if you can spare the time. One of these," he waved his hand at the technicians, who were busy tidying up. "One of these can return the specimen to your laboratory."

"I should be much honoured." Dr Mushni managed an

even lower bow and his face turned quite purple with pleasure. Valerie was glad that whatever it was she had produced on all that paper was going to be to his advantage. Specially when she was going to be leaving so soon. She kept her eyes down and her face expressionless as she was led along the passage, across the foyer and down the opposite corridor to Dr Mushni's lab.

The technician pushed her inside and locked the door. She could hear his heavy and uninterested feet plodding away into the distance. She leaned against the door and took a deep and shaky breath. Her hands were sticky and her knees felt wobbly.

She became aware of a steady rap-tapping from somewhere in the lab. Oh, my goodness. It was Isnek Ansnek signalling from inside the cupboard. She ran over and opened the door. "I'm so sorry!"

"Where *have* you been? I couldn't push open the door from the ridiculous position I have been forced to lie in all day. Overslept, I suppose? Talk about lack of consideration. I should have left last night as I originally planned. Well, don't just stand there. Help me out."

Valerie burst into tears, leaning against the counter, her tears splashing down unheeded.

"Watch out!" Mr Ansnek crept smartly out of the cupboard and jumped to one side. "Don't splash me. I've warned you about that before. You are the wettest young person I have ever encountered. What's the matter now?"

Valerie explained and Mr Ansnek apologized handsomely. "I am too hasty sometimes. I admit it. But no harm done, I hope. So dry yourself and let's leave." He moved on his long black legs along the rows of drawers, selecting tools with immense speed. Valerie left him to it and put on the Institute coveralls that she had found in one of the cupboards. They were almost the right length when she turned back the cuffs to her knees, only twice as wide, but they looked fairly presentable after she had tied the belt round her waist. It didn't actually make her look anything like a popeye, but from a distance the colour would seem familiar, if she should be seen. At least it wasn't as glaringly obvious as her pale blue jumpsuit.

She stuffed the dry food she'd saved into the front of her coveralls. Frank would be glad of real food after that horrible-looking slop. Even thinking about the fact that she would soon be seeing him made her feel happy, and the terror of the last few hours faded into a faint fluttering in her stomach.

She watched Mr Ansnek as he carefully melted the material from around the frame of the window. He gave it a gentle push and the whole unit, glass, mesh and bars, began to slide out. He grasped it and lowered it carefully to the ground outside.

"Quietly now," he whispered, and gave Valerie a boost onto the sill. She climbed neatly through and jumped down to one side, well away from the window unit. Mr Ansnek followed her, looking like a black stiff-jointed insect, and together they lifted up the window unit and pushed it back into place. The melted plastic was still sticky and the unit stayed in position. To the casual glance it would seem never to have been disturbed.

Valerie looked around, her heart pounding. There was nobody about. The night was very dark, unlit by any moon, and the stars themselves were faint and quite unfamiliar. Set about the grounds of the Institute were lamp standards, each casting a circle of golden light. In places the circles intersected each other. In others there were narrow paths of shadow lying between them.

Along these shadowy paths crept Valerie and Isnek Ansnek, the one a small bundle in bright yellow, the other as thin as a twig, as black as the shadows around him. The laboratory window had faced the back of the Institute, and as quickly and quietly as they could they moved away from the buildings through neatly laid-out grounds.

After about five minutes walking Valerie felt the path under her feet change from gravel to beaten dirt and then vanish altogether. The smooth lawns slowly became rank weed, knee-high, with a bitter smell that reminded Valerie of battery acid. Then they came to a belt of bushes, stretching as far as they could see into the darkness on either side. The lit area was now far behind.

At the sight of the bushes Valerie felt safer. Once among them they could not possibly be seen by anyone in the Institute. But they found the bushes had grown so closely together, making a dense jungle, that walking between them was impossible. They had to creep on hands and knees among the stems, beneath the intertwined branches. This slowed them down, but not by much.

It seemed a very long time, though, before the bushes stopped and Valerie was able to stand up again, her legs aching at the unaccustomed exercise. They had come to a wall, very smooth, made of the same kind of plastic stuff that formed the roads. Valerie reached up as far as her fingers would stretch, but she couldn't feel the top and there wasn't as much as a fingernail hold in that smoothness.

She turned in despair to Isnek Ansnek. Without hesitation he reached into his bag of tools, shaped a hook with fingers that were themselves tools, fastened the hook to a thin line of cord and tossed it up into the darkness. There was a tinkle and a faint scuttering noise, like birds' claws on stone. He flipped it back as if he were fishing and tried again. On the third cast the hook held firm.

With the cord dangling over his shoulder Isnek Ansnek walked up the wall, paying out the line through his powerful fingers. When he was astride the top Valerie could see his black feet dangling just above her head. "Come on," he whispered, and Valerie spat on her hands and rubbed them on her coveralls, grasped the cord and began to scramble up the slippery wall.

She was much noisier than the robot and by the time she was sitting astride the wall beside him she was out of breath and her hands were stinging where the thin cord had cut into them. The wall was smooth on top and wide enough to sit on comfortably. She wriggled around until her legs were dangling over the far side and looked down.

Sloping away below them, as neat and small from this angle as an architect's model, was the Zoo. They were on the highest point, and below them the landscape fell away in a series of curves, partly made of natural rock, partly built from buttresses of brick. Between these terraces wound paths that came together and separated as each path led past a different habitat.

It was a new and puzzling perspective, which made the familiar completely strange. The paths were marked with lights, set low along their sides and shaded downward, so that a spider's web of light overlay the dark slope. There seemed to be no other lights. Valerie wished she had cat's eyes. How was she ever going to find Frank? She looked up at the alien sky. There were still no moons. Perhaps this planet had none. The stars were few for, like a black veil, a swathe of interstellar dust lay across the sky just in the place where one would expect to see the crowded stars of the Milky Way.

Isnek Ansnek nudged her. "Where is the cage where your brother is imprisoned?" he whispered close against her ear.

"I don't know. I can't tell. It all looks so different from up here and in the dark."

Isnek tutted disapprovingly and she whispered hotly, "I'm not stupid. I know exactly where it is from the main entrance. Only not from up here."

"Sssh. Then we had better get down to the main entrance and work back from there." He twitched the rope over the wall and made Valerie slide down it ahead of him. Then he slithered neatly down after her, landing with a faint metallic jangle. He flicked the rope and the hook sailed through the air.

Valerie ducked.

"Sorry," he said. "Heads!"

When the rope was stowed away they started down the slope. They had to force their way through another barrier of bushes before they came to the first path. It was a blessed relief to make good speed downhill, and the brick pavement was silent and smooth under their feet.

Once the whine of a motor broke the silence and they dived for the bushes beside the road and lay among the twisted roots while a low one-person car shot by. Valerie caught a quick glimpse of the driver, dressed in yellow coveralls like hers and wearing a large pair of goggles.

"Probably infra-red," whispered Isnek Ansnek in her ear. "So that he can see in the dark. I hope he doesn't catch our trail."

Valerie lay still, willing herself not to move or breathe, nor to get hot and bothered either, as the car turned at the top and began to descend again. Her eyes on the twisted roots of the bushes, she found she was staring into the twelve green eye-spots of an enormous spider-like creature, and she jumped and bit back a yell.

"Be still!" hissed Isnek Ansnek.

The whine of the car faded. Obviously they had not left a noticeable heat trail on the path for the guard to pick up. Thankfully Valerie wriggled out from under the bush and shook herself, just in case there should be any more of those spider things lurking. The lamps which lined the low parapets gave a comforting orange glow and Valerie walked close to them and kept an eye out for any movement in the bushes.

The lights stopped and there was darkness, like a bottomless pool, directly ahead of them. When they got close they could just see that it was a walled habitat with shadowy lumps that were creatures from some other planet, dreaming of their own sky and their own trees and grass. Once they passed the habitat, the lit path continued. After a time it divided, one part swinging far over to the right, the other descending in a series of steps. The choice was easy. They took the steep path, down the steps. It was quicker and they wouldn't be surprised by the night patrol.

"We must hurry," Isnek Ansnek hissed. "I do not know how soon the white sun rises, but I know that at the present time it is ahead of the red sun. Once it is risen we will no longer have the darkness to hide us."

"I am hurrying," Valerie whispered back in a breathless angry panic. "The best I can. But I've never been in this part of the Zoo before and everything's muddled and backwards."

"Keep your shirt on," Isnek replied amiably. Valerie felt giggles spurting up inside her as she wondered where he'd picked up such an antiquated expression.

She ran full tilt into a sign post and bruised her nose painfully. The arms sticking out from it obviously said things like 'The Monkey House' or 'This way to the Elephants'. If only I had a torch, she thought, rubbing her nose, I could read them. But she didn't know how Frank would be labelled anyway.

The path ran into a wide area and directly ahead was the faint familiar shape of a kiosk that sold, Valerie remembered, brightly coloured food and drink. Just the other side of that...

"Quick, Mr Ansnek, I've found it!" She ran around the kiosk and there, sure enough, was the plain cage with nothing in it but the den over in the right hand corner that Frank had built. She ran over and whispered between the bars. "Frank, wake up! It's me."

There was no sound but a distant howl. She daren't raise her voice in case the guards should hear. There were no bushes in the paved square for them to dive behind if someone should suddenly appear. There might be guards on foot, too, she thought. You'd have no warning at all...

A heavy hand fell on her shoulder and she just managed to swallow a hearty scream. She turned. It was only Isnek Ansnek. "Don't *ever* do that again," she managed to say faintly. "You nearly gave me a heart attack."

"Sorry. Why are you standing there?"

"I was trying to waken Frank. Only he always did sleep like the dead, and I'm afraid to talk any louder."

"Wouldn't it be more efficient for you to go into the cage and waken him from inside?"

"Yes, of course it would, but..."

"Then I'll unlock the door for you." He stalked around to the front. "You had only to ask," he reproved as he fiddled with the lock.

In less time than it would have taken her to find the right key on a ring, he had the door open. Valerie scrambled in and ran quietly across the straw-strewn floor to the den at the back.

It smelt awful, much worse than a pigsty. Well, no wonder, with no washing or sanitary arrangements. In fact I've seen pigs treated better, she thought indignantly. She took a deep breath, crept into the hovel and shook Frank's shoulder, talking softly all the time.

"Sssh! It's me. Val. Frank, wake up. We're getting out of here. Come on now, do wake up."

He finally came awake without yelling and she pulled his arm until he stumbled out of the hut after her. "Val, is it really you? It can't be. I'm dreaming again... Lord, they've put that awful drug in my food... None of it's real."

He put his hands over his hairy face and cringed away from her in a way that made Valerie want to cry, it was so completely unlike Frank. She caught hold of his arms and shook him. "Listen, Frank, it's really me. I'm here."

His face changed and his arms went round her in a weak version of the old bear hug he used to give her. Then- ...was he crying? *Frank*?

Over his shoulder she saw the flash of lights on the hill. She could hear the whine of the guard's car. "Isnek!" she hissed, and saw the gate of the cage swing silently shut. "Frank, lie down! Quick, don't say a word." She pushed him to the floor of the cage and crouched down by him, her face buried in his horribly smelly shoulder. Her heart thumped like a drum.

The car whined slowly down the zigzag road, circled the square and disappeared along the path that led towards the main gate.

Would he turn at once and come back? Perhaps he would go into the little ticket office, rest, write a report, have a hot drink...

Or perhaps he wouldn't. There are times when luck is the only thing left to count on. This was one of them. She rolled off Frank and helped him to his feet. The cage door swung open and Isnek Ansnek silently appeared, ready to help them down.

Frank drew back as the black metal hand reached out. "What the...?"

"Frank, this is Isnek Ansnek," Valerie whispered. "He's helping us escape." It was the oddest introduction she had ever made. "I'll explain later, but we've got to get out of here before the sun rises."

Frank took Isnek's hand, swung down from the cage

and turned to help Valerie. Then they ran, over to the right, away from the main gate, away from the city, towards the mountains. Suddenly it was getting easier to see. With the lurch of fear she realised that dawn was coming, the false dawn of the white sun, distant, but brighter than ten moons.

Frank saw her look and nodded grimly. Together they ran. Where paths looped in a leisurely way around beds of shrubs and flowers they took short cuts across the middle. Once, when they came to a low wall, Valerie recklessly flung her leg over it, but Frank pulled her back. "Val, watch out!"

She looked down and saw in the shadowy ditch beyond the wall a writhing entwining movement. With a menacing hiss a spade-shaped head reared up. She drew back with a gasp of terror and clung to Frank's arm.

"It's okay, Val." Frank gave her a quick hug and they ran on. She noticed that he was limping quite badly. His face glistened with sweat, white in the dawn light.

"Your leg — oh, Frank, you're hurt."

"Just a run-in with my keeper," he panted. "Put my knee out. It's all right. I'll manage."

But when they reached the perimeter wall he could not climb the rope unaided. Valerie had to scramble up and haul him from above while Isnek boosted him from below. They slid down the rope on the far side and Frank landed clumsily with a gasp of pain.

"Oh, dear. Are you going to be able to walk?"

"Have to, won't I?" He looked grimly over his shoulder. "I won't go back to that. I'd sooner be dead."

"Come on then. Lean on my shoulder."

They set off across rough grey-brown grass that grew in coarse tufts in the stony soil. It was not a place to hurry, even under the best of conditions. With Valerie and Isnek Ansnek helping Frank, their progress was painfully slow.

Valerie found herself looking back over her shoulder at the long line of the Zoo wall, which seemed to get no farther away, no matter how they struggled.

"I did lock the cage. There is no reason for your brother to be missed before the morning feeding," Isnek said as she glanced back for the tenth time.

"I'll be missed before that," she reminded him. "Dr Mushni always brings me my breakfast as soon as the red sun rises. We've got to be a long way away before that. But I don't see how..."

They struggled to the top of a gentle rise and found they were looking across a shallow valley to parkland that stretched away to distant foothills and a horizon rimmed with mountains. Frank stopped, easing the weight off his bad leg. "Over there. We won't really be safe until we get there."

"How can we possibly...?" Valerie wailed.

"There are buildings in that clump of trees." Isnek pointed. "I will go down and see if I can find a vehicle for our use. Meet me at the road. Over there, by that purple tree."

"Yes, all right. Frank, can you make it that far with just my help?"

"Sure. Of course. Not to worry, little sister."

Isnek dropped lightly down onto the wiry turf below the crest of the hill. His spidery legs moved fast and neatly. He waved them on. "Hurry! Under the purple tree."

With Frank's arm unbearably heavy across her shoulder, Valerie stumbled over the coarse spiky grass towards the road on their left. The sky was pinky-orange. Above the second sun shone harsh and white. Soon popeyes would be getting up, making breakfast, looking out of their windows...

Her ankle turned in a hidden hole and they both went over with a thump that knocked the wind out of her. She wheezed and gasped and struggled to her knees. Frank's face was an awful greenish colour.

"Oh, Frank, that was all my fault. I'm so sorry."

He managed a smile. "Silly billy. You're doing fine. Come on, give us a hand up, there's a good girl."

He didn't even squeak when she hauled him to his feet and they set out once more. The road seemed as far away as ever.

As she stared longingly at it, two small sparks of light appeared, moving towards them from the city. Oh, don't let them be looking this way, she prayed silently.

"Frank, down!"

Together they dropped into the rough grass and crouched, holding each other. Even in the terror of the moment Valerie felt an odd kind of happiness. At least they were together now. Whatever awfulness happened they weren't alone any more.

The engine whine came close and then faded. They looked up cautiously to see two small tail lights vanish up the road that led towards the distant mountains. They hadn't been seen.

The red glow of the rising sun was like the reflection of a forest fire in the sky ahead. With the strength of desperation Valerie hauled Frank to his feet and pulled his arm over her shoulder. She hung onto his waist with her free hand.

"Come on. We'll make it."

By the time they finally reached the purple cabbage tree sweat was running down Valerie's face and Frank was stumbling beside her, his eyes closed, his teeth biting his lower lip. Isnek appeared from the shadows and helped her lift Frank into the high back of the boxy open car the robot had commandeered. Valerie tried to make him comfortable with his feet up on the wide seat. Isnek helped her up the high step into the front.

"Can you really drive this thing? It looks awfully complicated."

"It is certainly a very primitive design and overlarge for me. But I can manage it, in spite of this collection of knobs. It is interesting to note that the more advanced cultures have the simplest machinery. I remember once being driven in a car that was guided purely by thought waves. Elegant, I can tell you. But the driver really had to keep his mind on his job."

He swerved madly round a curve, passed the turn-off to the house from where he had stolen the car, and set off across the undulating plain.

When the red sun finally popped up above the mountains ahead they were still crossing the plain. They had not seen another car nor any further buildings. Valerie sat on the edge of her seat, terrified that at any moment a popeye would appear. The further away from danger they got, the more afraid she was of their recapture. Prison had been hard to cope with before. Now it would be quite unbearable.

She looked back at Frank. He'd fallen asleep, with his head bouncing gently against the orange upholstery. His colour was a little better. Dear Frank. She felt she had never really appreciated him before. Now they were together all they had to do was to make a plan to find Susan and get her away from her fat popeye owner. And then what? Somehow get off this horrible planet. How?

I won't worry about it now, she told herself firmly. Together we'll manage. And if we can't get away at least we'll be free, living together in the mountains. Then a sudden picture of Mother and Father alone on Eden without any of them came into her mind and she stifled a sob.

She turned around again, blinking furiously, and saw the air tremble. She rubbed her eyes and stared. For a minute it had seemed as if a column of air had joined the sky to the earth. Then it was gone. Like a mirage on a hot desert day. Only this planet wasn't hot and this place wasn't a desert.

"What was *that*?"

"I am not sure, but..." Isnek's voice was different, almost as if he were excited. But robots don't have emotions, do they? "It could be the matter transmitter I am looking for. In fact..." He said no more, but the next time a yellow road intersected the purple one on which they were travelling, he yanked the steering wheel over so suddenly that Valerie was thrown against his shoulder.

"Sorry," was all he said, and drove fast until they came to a purple road. Isnek turned left. Now the place where the shimmer had appeared was directly ahead of them. Shortly afterwards they approached a heavy forest that grew like a blanket over the low hills to their left. It was lush and green, different from any vegetation Valerie had seen on this planet. Above and beyond it was the tip of a white tower.

"That place...do you think it's got something to do with the shimmer?"

Isnek answered slowly. "I think that..."

She interrupted him with a scream. "There's a car coming down the road. Oh, quick!"

But Isnek had already seen and slowed down. He turned the car off the road into the forest, which at this point crowded against the highway on their left. They bumped slowly along between the trees until they came to a small glade. Isnek turned off the engine and hopped out.

"Where are you going?"

"Back to the road to take a look. The car may be coming from that place. There seems to be no other buildings around. In fact the whole area is strangely deserted."

"Wait a minute. I'm coming too." Valerie jumped out. Frank still slept on the back seat. She hesitated, not wanting to leave him alone. There was something very spooky about the shadows of the forest. The darkness seemed to be full of unknown shapes and you could almost fancy that you could hear the trees breathe. She shivered. "Wait for me!"

She followed Isnek along the trail that the car treads had made. The turf was spongy beneath their feet. It had been torn where the treads had dug in and moisture was oozing out to fill the scars they had made. It was all very green and lush and still.

Isnek crouched close to the road, near enough to pitch a stone onto its purple surface, and Valerie knelt beside him. The trees behind them sighed and the ground seemed to move very slightly. Valerie felt the skin on her arms prickle and the hair rise at the nape of her neck. She wanted to grab Isnek's hand, but that would be too ridiculous for words.

The distant putt-putt turned to a roar. They had a quick glimpse of a big squarish truck, the driver, paler than normal, his eye tentacles fully extended, crouched over the wheel. They glimpsed a cage and in it a shape, so unfamiliar that Valerie could make no sense of it at all. Then the road was empty. The putt-putt faded to a hum.

Silence crowded back. Silence that was filled with the slow heavy breathing of the trees and the faint movement of the turf beneath their feet. Valerie looked up into the sky, up at the tree tops. There was not a breath of wind.

"Isnek, there's something funny about this forest."

"I too sense something not right." He turned and walked rapidly back between the trees to the place where they had parked the car, Valerie running after him. The tracks she had followed before were gone.

"You've come the wrong way." She pointed to the ground.

"No. The car is directly ahead of..." Isnek stopped. The clearing was empty.

"I *told* you."

"This *is* the place. I do not make that kind of mistake."

"You must have. The car's not here. Frank wouldn't have driven off. And anyway we'd have heard the engine." She ran to the left, between trees that seemed to crowd around her. There was another clearing just ahead, very like the first. It too was empty.

"Wait, Valerie. You will only lose your way. There is something wrong with this forest. It is not what it seems. Wait. Don't move."

Valerie waited obediently, standing in the middle of the clearing. Her eyes stared at the shadows, willing them to be still. Her hands were sweating and she rubbed them impatiently against her coveralls. Something tickled her ankles.

She looked down. The green turf was slowly creeping over her feet. Her shoes were completely hidden, and it was starting to grow up her ankles. She screamed and kicked out wildly. One foot and then the other. She leapt from the centre of the clearing towards where Isnek Ansnek was coming towards her.

"Look." She pointed, clutching at him. Two red holes marked the centre of the clearing where she had been standing. Two holes like wounds. While she stared the turf slowly closed over the damage.

"The car." She stared at Isnek. "And Frank. What has it done with him? What has the forest done to my brother?"

She burst into tears. The trees drew a little closer.

Six Plus One

Valerie tripped over a wiry root of the low scrub that covered the dry ground. She picked herself up and stumbled on after Isnek Ansnek. Her hands were swollen and her ankles scratched and bruised — this was not the first time she had fallen — but she didn't notice the pain.

Frank was dead . . . She remembered how kind he'd been when she had first started school and had a miserable time settling in. There was that terrific day when just the two of them had taken the high-speed mono to Dream City; he'd taken her to every single exhibit from Prehistoric Earth to a trip through a Black Hole. Now he was gone, devoured by that alien forest. She would never see him again. It was almost too much to bear.

But there was a worse pain. It was *her* fault. She had left him sleeping in the car and run after Isnek Ansnek because she didn't want to wait alone in the spooky forest. She'd been a rotten little scaredy cat and it was all her fault. If only . . . She tripped over another root and fell flat on her face.

After they had fled the devouring forest she and the robot had run along the purple road until they came to the yellow crossroad where the white tower stood. The crossroads marked the boundary of the forest, which crowded greedily against the margins of the roads, as if it would have grown over them if it could.

Once past the intersection they had taken to the open country of rough scrubby hills and occasional grass-lined valleys with streams wandering along the bottom of them. The tableland turned slowly into foothills, and the distant mountains came slowly nearer as they walked. Where Mr Ansnek was going and how long he intended to go on walking Valerie did not know. It did not matter. He was her only friend, her last link with loving on this awful planet, and she wasn't going to let him out of her sight.

The ground was rising more steeply now, the beginning of the true foothills. The far mountains flared in the reflection of the setting sun. Mr Ansnek walked on, his steady pace unchanging. Valerie stumbled after him. I will lift up mine eyes to the hills from whence comes my salvation. The words came into her mind and she walked to their rhythm. Ouch! She fell and picked herself up again. From whence comes my salvation ... my salvation ...

It was getting dark. Would he walk all night? How could she follow him then? His black body vanished into the shadows as they trudged down a slope into a valley folded between two hills. There were some trees down there, not the awful alien ones but familiar cabbage-shaped clumps. Bushes too, with spreading branches and leathery leaves of brownish purple. There was a stream, and on the far side a smooth rocky slope still warm from the sun.

Isnek Ansnek stepped fastidiously from stone to stone, careful not to get his feet wet. Valerie splashed blindly after him through the water, ready to trudge on up the next slope. He stopped her.

"I think you are tired. We will rest here."

She slumped to the ground like a puppet with its strings cut.

"Are you not thirsty? My sensors tell me that the water is safe for human consumption."

Thirsty? Valerie licked her cracked lips. Her throat was like sand. She fell forward on her stomach so that her face was just above the stream and splashed the water into her mouth with her hands. It had a strong metallic taste, but she drank and drank until Isnek Ansnek pulled her away and made her stop.

"Perhaps you are hungry? I can scan for something edible."

Valerie shuddered and shook her head. She wanted nothing that came from this cannibal planet that had taken Frank. She lay back on the sun-warmed rock, her arms wrapped across her chest, and stared up at the dark sky, the slowly emerging unfamiliar stars. Somewhere out there in the immensity of galactic space was Eden. Was DeePeeThree. But where? Would she ever see home again? See Mother and Father? She stared up at the loneliness of space with dry burning eyes and she felt as empty as the sky.

After a long time she fell asleep and only then, in her dreaming, did tears trickle from the corners of her eyes and run down onto the red rock. Isnek put his hand out to waken her, but changed his mind and let her sleep on.

Valerie woke after a long sleep, cosy under a light blanket. Her eyes still shut, she stretched, enjoying the freedom of fresh air and open sky instead of the stuffiness of the cupboard bed in Dr Mushni's laboratory. She felt warm and happy. Wow, what a dumb dream!

She opened her eyes to stare up into the hard white spot that was this planet's secondary sun. Over to her left the primary was just rising, huge and red. Not a dream after all. She screwed up her eyes and pulled the blanket over her face, while the events of the day before raced across her mind. The escape. The Zoo. Freeing Frank. The forest...

It wasn't true. It couldn't be true. Frank couldn't really

be dead—not Frank. Maybe it hadn't really happened...
But the pain inside her told her that it had. She was alone.

She pushed the corner of the blanket into her mouth to
stop herself from screaming out loud and going on screaming and screaming until she had no voice left. She rolled
into a tight bundle with the pain that was inside her in the
middle of it. Oh, please God take it away. Please let it all
be a dream...

Through the pain she felt the blanket against her face, an
unfamiliar softness on this harsh planet. She smelt a
strange exotic scent and sat up suddenly, fully awake. She
and Mr Ansnek had brought nothing with them in their
escape from the forest except the tools he had carried on
his person. Where had this blanket come from?

It was a shawl, she realized, when she looked at it
properly, finely woven of white and gold yarn, as fine as a
spider's web, as warm as *zenib*'s wool. She stretched it
between her hands and stared in amazement at the design,
a picture of slender willow-like trees and elegant birds with
trailing tail feathers. It had never been made on this planet,
never in a million years!

She scrambled to her feet and looked round for Isnek
Ansnek. The valley was deserted. She was quite alone.
"Mr Ansnek! Mr Ansnek, where are you?" Her heart
thumped.

He appeared on the hill above her and picked his way
down over the bare rock to where she stood. "What a lot
of sleep your body requires. It must be most inconvenient
for you."

She was so glad to see him she could have hugged his
black metal body. "Oh, Isnek, I thought you'd left me.
Look, where did this come from?" She held out the shawl.

"Beautiful work, is it not? From Persis, I believe."

She stamped her foot. "You must know I didn't mean
that. Where did it come from *here*."

"You were shivering. One of our rescuers covered you with it. I have been waiting for a considerable time to take you to them."

"Our..." Valerie swallowed. "You mean there are people from Persis *here*?"

"One person. The others are from different Federation planets. Six in all."

"You've seen them yourself? They were *here*, while I was asleep?"

"I met two of them. It seemed wise to let you sleep on. They went back to their home to tell the others and to prepare food."

Home. Food. In spite of her misery Valerie felt a little better. Her stomach tightened and her mouth began to water. How long since she'd had a decent meal? She'd forgotten. "Let's go then, quickly. Oh, quick!" She wrapped the white and gold shawl around her shoulders and followed Isnek Ansnek over the hill.

If they had walked on for only another hour the previous evening they would have come directly upon the strangers' hiding place, though they would probably have walked right past it in the dark. Even in full daylight it was not easy to see. Many years before a hillside had fallen away, and in the base of the cliff that remained were caves, some as small as burrows, some as big as rooms.

In front of one of them now burned a small bright fire. There were three humans standing by the fire, two men and a woman. Three others also, humanoid perhaps, but definitely not of Earth origin. Six. Hadn't Isnek Ansnek said there were six of them? Who was the seventh? A human, squatting by the fire, spooning food into his hairy face as if he hadn't eaten in months.

She stopped walking and stared, swallowed and blinked her eyes. Maybe she was seeing things because she so badly wanted to. She ran forward. It was him. It really was! She slithered down the scree-covered slope and ran across the valley bottom towards the cliff base.

"Frank! Oh, Frank, you're alive!"

He looked up at her voice, threw down the dish and limped down to meet her where a stream meandered across the valley bottom. They hugged and exclaimed and hugged again. Valerie couldn't stop crying, though she scrubbed her face with her hands to get rid of the tears. Frank laughed and said she was turning into a painted *wennatoo* from the mixture of dirt and tears. He helped her wash her face in the stream, and dried it with the corner of his shirt, a clean shirt that was not his own. There were tears in his eyes too, and he gave her another hug.

"Oh, Frank, it's like a miracle. How did you get here? I thought the forest had eaten you and it was all my fault because I left you sleeping and went after Mr Ansnek because I didn't want to be alone, it was so spooky, and..."

"Hey, don't start again. You're soaking my shirt. It wasn't your fault, silly. Who would have expected a people-eating forest? It was a near thing though. If Tenkle and Mani hadn't been watching the Tower, I would never have got out, not with my gammy knee."

"Tenkle and Mani?"

"Up there. You'll meet them all in a minute. Well, I woke up with this extraordinary heavy feeling in my legs—I thought I was dreaming—and the car had nearly gone under the turf and the grass was climbing over the car doors and across my knees. It was like trying to escape from quicksand. I didn't know what had happened to you two and I was afraid to yell in case the fatties were somewhere around and you were hiding from them."

"Fatties? Oh, yes. *I* call them popeyes. Go on."

"Mani and Tenkle appeared just then. He's the great

strong chap up there. He pulled me out like a cork out of a bottle and slung me over his shoulder and whisked me out of the forest and over the hills to here."

"Here?"

"Home of a sort to other escapees from the Zoo. Some of them have been here for ages, you know."

"Oh, Frank!"

"What's up?"

"You said 'ages'. And no one's managed to escape? Maybe there isn't any way off the planet. Maybe we're stuck..."

"Steady. What you need is a hot meal. Come on. Let's meet the others and get some food into you. It's funny stuff, but better than the Zoo slop, I can tell you."

Frank limped up the slope, his arm over Valerie's shoulder, talking all the time. "You'll have to tell me what's been happening to you and how you latched on to that robot fellow. And how you found me. That was a marvel! I got the shock of my life when you suddenly appeared last night. At first I thought I'd gone mad, you know. Nasty feeling. But what an answer to prayer you were! I'd about given up, I'll tell you."

"When you and Susan didn't come out of the maze, I went in after you," Valerie explained. She didn't want to tell Frank her exact feelings as she had followed them. After all, it was light years away in space and time. What a selfish little stupid I was, she thought, and blushed for her other self.

"Go on."

Valerie explained how she'd fooled Dr Mushni and assembled Isnek Ansnek. By the time she had finished they had reached the ridge beneath the cliff where the others were waiting to meet her.

"You're a ruddy little marvel." Frank gave her a hug that made her feel warm right down to her blistered feet.

"Hey, everyone, come and meet my rescuer. My very special sister, Valerie!"

After a wonderful, though peculiar, feast, they held a council of war.

"We've kept a watch of sorts on the White Tower ever since we came together after our separate escapes." Doil, the young scientist from Tabara, explained. He had wild rusty red hair and beard, and his white lab suit was worn through at the knees and elbows. He looked like the video of the Count of Monte Cristo. Valerie wondered how long *he*'d been a prisoner. "We believe that the disturbances, that shimmering in the air above the White Tower, is a disruption of the gravitational or magnetic field. These disturbances only seem to occur when the white and red star are in a certain position in the sky relative to the Tower. We think that the forces developed by these two suns revolving around each other cause tensions which are used to power the Matter Transmitter — what you called the Space Trap."

"And it's in the White Tower."

"Yes, it's like a ruddy great vacuum cleaner. They point the nozzle at certain spots on a planet and suck up whatever is unlucky enough to be there," Tenkle interrupted. He was a big man, deeply tanned, with muscles that looked as if they were capable of wrestling a mammoth to the ground.

"Then they put whatever they've caught in a cage and take it down to the city?" Valerie remembered her lurching trip down the purple highway.

"But knowing how the receiver works isn't going to help us get off the planet," Frank objected.

"All knowledge is potentially useful," Doil said flatly and Isnek Ansnek nodded agreement.

Frank looked obstinate. He'd had the same argument with Dad over taking Latin and Greek as well as Earth

English and Intergalactic. Before an argument could start Valerie interrupted, "Are you sure the Tower *is* only a receiver?"

Everyone stared at her and she blushed.

"We have never observed objects being taken into the Tower and not returning to the town. But you're quite right. We should not make assumptions."

"You see," Valerie went on, "it seemed at the time that the stone pyramid and the maze didn't belong on DeePeeThree. And I saw the popeye symbol for 'zoo' on some of the thorn bushes. Looking back it's obvious that the maze was planted as a trap. There was nothing else interesting on the planet. Sooner or later an intelligent being would explore that maze."

"So?" Donald wrinkled his forehead.

"The popeyes must have gone to DeePeeThree to build the pyramid and plant the maze, mustn't they? Yet they don't seem to have space craft. And anyway, the Federation Police would have caught them for violating planetary space. How did they get there to set the trap?"

"Good thinking, Val. Is our 'trap' anything like yours?" He turned to the others.

"On Persis, in my father's garden, is a small archway," Mani spoke quietly. She wore the shawl Valerie had returned over her dark hair and across one shoulder. Beneath it her gold dress shimmered in the red sun. "It is not made of the same stone as the house or the little temple or the fountain, not even of the same stone as the great wall that surrounds the estate, and that is the oldest of all. It was supposed the gods must have placed it there. But was it placed there by these creatures? And how? I was meditating beneath it one afternoon when I was brought to . . . to this place." She drew the shawl closely about her head and moved into the shadows.

Tenkle grunted. "My experience was very different. I

was in the wild animal sanctuary on the northern island of Nakhan. There have been many disappearances of rare animals and we could make no sense of what the natives told us. So the government sent me there. I'm a game warden now, used to be a soldier. My job, to shoot to kill anyone caught stealing the animals.

"Well, I'd been up there many days, no clues, saw no one. Then one day, right in front of my eyes, a *scramaloupe* disappeared. You ever seen a scramaloupe? Well, they're the size of a small house, rare beasts and handsome, with curved tusks and red and grey stripes. I had this one in my binoculars. Minding his own business, grazing in a clearing. Then he was gone. I swear I didn't even blink, and he was gone!

"Got over to where I'd seen him as fast as I could. Nothing there, of course. Just a glade full of merryflowers and the air shimmery, like desert heat, though under the giant trees it was quite cool. I rushed into the glade and the next thing I know there's an inside-out upside-down feeling and I'm in a cage driving along that damn purple highway."

After a pause Frank said, "Er...I'm not sure what the point of that story is?"

"Exactly," Tenkle said triumphantly. "Interesting story, but no point. It was just a glade of merryflowers, after all. No trap. Why are we wasting our time on history instead of planning how to get out of here?"

"We learn from history."

"I don't see..."

"The experience of Mani and our friends from Eden suggests that the popeyes *did* travel to their planets some time in the past and place artifacts there, buildings, mazes, whatever. On Nakhan they didn't have to. To catch a scramaloupe all you need is a glade full of merryflowers."

"Coincidence."

"I don't think so," Mani spoke again. "The trap may be the same, but the bait is selective, almost as if they knew. On my planet a meditation place. On DeePeeThree a maze to attract explorers. On Nakhan..." she shrugged her thin shoulders, "on Nakhan a glade of merryflowers."

"So it's very likely that the White Tower *can* transmit matter as well as receive it," Doil said firmly as Tenkle opened his mouth. "How did they know enough about our planets to use the right, the enticing bait?"

"I think the baiting took place a long time ago, and now they just use what they've got." Valerie surprised herself by saying. "The popeyes are awfully lazy, and the ones I've met are not a bit clever about psychology and stuff like that. It's...well it seems to me maybe an earlier culture built the trap, and now these popeyes are just using it—wasting it really, when you think of letting specimens go as pets. And they were arguing over money," she remembered, "almost as if the Transmitter wasn't important, not compared with the Zoo; as if they didn't really understand any more what they'd got."

Doil looked excited. He got up and began to prowl up and down. "Just using an old discovery. Not building on it...And now they're lazy. So they're probably not using the Transmitter to discover new planets at all. If we knew where all their traps were we could find the position of this system, roughly at least, and put an end to it."

"Once we're off this planet," said Frank practically.

One of the humanoids grunted in what seemed to be laughter.

"Where do these others come from?" Valerie asked. "Do they speak Intergalactic?"

"Yes, we do." The voice from the big hairy creature was a growl, with a thick accent, hard to understand. "We are members of Federation. From Plabskitsa. My wife is named Filio and I am Sturpis. This person communicate only by touch." He pointed to the third humanoid, who looked like a large pink sphere with arms and legs.

Valerie held out a timid hand. At once a fleshy finger reached out to touch the tip of her forefinger. "I am so happy to meet you," a voice spoke in Valerie's head, and she knew — though how could she? — that this pink lump was a girl not much older than herself. "I am Fifth Daughter from blue-roof house on big island of planet that Federation call Japonica. We do not use names much ourselves, excuse me. You talk of mode of arriving at this place? I was standing on bridge that led to sacred temple when I was brought here. Very bad place. Full of evil thoughts."

"I don't remember what the inside of the White Tower was like. Do any of you?" Valerie asked and they all shook their heads.

"So none of us even know what the Matter Transmitter looks like, much less how it works?"

"Which is exactly why we're going to have to find out as much as we can about the Tower. Up close."

"But we've had a watch on it almost every day, Doil. That's how Mani and I found Frank. We were up on the ridge watching the Tower and we saw the trees begin to move. So we went to have a look. There was Frank up to his hips in turf, looking mighty surprised." He grinned at the memory.

Valerie shuddered. "Don't! I can't think why you didn't see us. We couldn't have been far off."

Tenkle chuckled. "I did. Between the trees. I saw your coveralls and thought you were popeyes. Never moved so quietly and quickly in my life."

"We're getting off the subject. My suggestion is that we move our entire camp down to the Tower and watch it day and night. Time the movement of the popeyes. Find a way of getting in. There *must* be a weak link in the system somewhere."

"We've got to be careful of that forest."

"It's still confined by the roads. The Tower side is perfectly safe."

"We'd be awfully visible camping down there," Tenkle objected, looking up at the snug caves in the cliffs above them.

"I admit it'll be more dangerous than where we are now. Look, everyone. We've got two choices. We can go on living here in reasonable comfort and continue to send someone down every day or so to watch the Tower. We've been doing that for a year and we've learned little. Or we can all go, watch the Tower every single moment, day and night, and risk being spotted. I think we should vote on it."

"I vote we go."

"I agree. We have waited long enough."

"Me too."

"And I."

"Very well."

"We also," growled Sturpis, and Fifth Daughter nodded her pink head.

They didn't move camp until the swelling in Frank's knee had gone down. Valerie enjoyed those days, which reminded her of camping trips into the State Parks back on Eden, when she was young. The caves were surprisingly comfortable, being fitted out with mattresses of dried grass, hammocks and mats of woven reeds, bowls and spoons hollowed out from roots and stones. But there seemed to be no regret when they finally packed up and moved.

Fifth Daughter said, "Every day we do nothing is a day lost to our family and friends. What are danger and discomfort if they bring us closer to home?"

The others must have felt the same, because they packed up and left without a backward glance, taking with them only the bare essentials.

"Water may be the greatest problem. This stream was a godsend, so close to the caves. We must find a place as close to the Tower as possible, but still near enough to fresh water and a place where we can risk lighting a fire just once a day. Our main food is the fungus flowers and they aren't eatable unless they're boiled."

"At least we won't be a day's march away from the Tower. That was a great waste of energy." Tenkle grew livelier with each step closer to danger. "If only I had my guns with me."

"Didn't you have them when you saw the scramaloupe vanish?

"Of course. It's damn odd."

"Perhaps the Transmitter rejects metals? That could be an important clue."

They trudged on in silence across the wiry scrub.

"My gold chains and ear-rings came through with me," Mani said at last.

"And my steel belt buckle," Frank remembered.

"I might remind you that I am all metal and I am here."

They stared in surprise at Isnek Ansnek and began to laugh. It was infectious and soon all of them were reeling through the scrub, mopping their eyes.

"All right then. Calm down," said Doil. "Where did Tenkle's weapons go?"

"If they pumped in sleeping gas or something as soon as specimens arrived, then they could tranfer the dangerous ones — like the wallaroon — to cages right away," Valerie suggested shyly.

"I think you've got it, Val. They'd take away any weapons at the same time."

"I'd give a lot to know where my guns are."

"Probably in some museum collection. I wonder how they're labelled?" Frank grinned at the outraged expression on Tenkle's face.

They found a camp two valleys away from the yellow highway, at a place where the purple highway veered off to the right, off to some other city, or maybe only to villages, since there was very little traffic on either of the roads.

"Maybe only government people have cars," guessed Frank. "If popeyes were free to travel, surely by now they'd be crowding around the Tower asking questions, and getting eaten up by the forest. Then there'd be no end of fuss."

"Maybe this area is restricted and the popeyes are all very law-abiding and obedient."

"Either way we can count on any traffic being hostile," Doil pointed out.

"Most logical," Isnek Ansnek approved.

Doil turned to him. "You've been very quiet. What is your opinion of our position and aims?"

"I see no purpose in talk with insufficient data. We need to know a great deal more about the Tower *and* the forest."

"The forest?"

"It is an anomaly. It does not belong."

Fifth Daughter wriggled and waved a pink hand at Valerie, who reached out to touch it.

"Oh dear, this is complicated. I think she's saying that if the forest is a living entity then it must be able to communicate with the different parts of itself. Remember how the trees all leaned towards us when we walked by, Isnek? It must have been warning the rest of itself. Well, Fifth Daughter thinks that if it does communicate with itself in some way, she may be able to overhear it . . . find out what it's doing here. It could be useful."

"It certainly could." Doil nodded.

"But does one stop to converse with the tiger?" asked Mani.

"It'll be awfully risky, Fifth Daughter."

"I'll go with her," Frank volunteered, but she shook her head and turned an even deeper shade of pink.

"She can't go alone. That's ridiculous."

"Oh, listen. She doesn't feel comfortable talking with men, she says. Or with Mani." Valerie stopped and gulped. "She...she says she'll only go and find out about the forest if I go with her."

7

The Entity Moab

The red sun had set and the alien night sky arched over the low hills. Beyond the ridge which hid their new camp only one more hill separated Valerie and Fifth Daughter from the White Tower. Valerie crept as quietly as she could up the rise, moving cautiously to avoid getting her ankles caught in the wiry roots and branches that sprawled across the slope. It was even more difficult at night.

Beside her, Fifth Daughter waddled on stumpy pink legs. If we have to run for it she'll never make it, thought Valerie bitterly. But she's my friend now and I'll have to wait for her and we'll both be captured again. Only this time it won't be kind Dr Mushni. We'll be sent to that basement room and turned back into molecules and atoms. I wish she wasn't my friend. I wish she didn't even like me. What's so special about me, after all? If only she'd liked Doil or Mani better, they'd be crawling up this hill now, getting tripped every other minute, and I'd be back at camp sleeping.

She fell over again, biting back the 'ouch' as the iron-hard roots grazed her ankles. When she got up it was to see Fifth Dauther at the top of the rise. Despite her rolypoly shape and stumpy legs she had moved with amazing speed and neatness and hadn't tripped once.

Valerie crept the last few metres on all fours and lay beside her. She felt ashamed at her thoughts and hoped that Fifth Daughter hadn't been able to read them. She remembered how Frank had protested at her being part of this enterprise, and the approval in his eyes when she'd said she must go. Well, here she was. So stop fussing, Valerie!

Below them the ground flattened towards the intersection of the purple and yellow roads, the purple almost invisible in the darkness. Both roads were completely deserted. The White Tower gleaming palely against the blackness of the carnivorous forest behind it. From a tall thin window set high in its wall Valerie could see the faint glow of reflected light. There was no sound nor movement from either within or without.

"You must be tired, Valerie," Fifth Daughter reached out a pudgy finger to touch her. "I come from a planet even denser than this one, so I feel as light as a feather here and walking is a pleasure."

The picture of the pink round humanoid as a feather was irresistible, and Valerie felt laughter rising inside her like soda pop. She tried to gulp it back but a giggle escaped. "Oh, I'm sorry. I didn't mean..."

"Don't worry. I find your shape exceedingly funny also. But these details don't interfere with our friendship, do they?"

"No, of course not," Valerie answered guiltily, remembering her disloyal thoughts as she'd climbed the slope.

"Valerie, I want to tell you a secret. Do you understand the significance of what I am called?"

"Fifth Daughter? Well, I suppose that's what you are."

A great sadness filled Valerie as the humanoid sighed. "It is much more than that. On Japonica a couple is permitted to have four children. If they are so unlucky as to have only girls, they may apply for special permission to have a fifth child, in the hope that this time fortune may smile on them and present them with a son."

Valerie worked this out. Then she exploded angrily.

"That's rotten. As if girls weren't every bit as important and just as useful."

Fifth Daughter smiled inwardly. "I knew you felt that way. That was why I wished us to be friends. You have struggled against injustice too, have you not?"

"Oh, I used to get sick of having to babysit Susan while Frank got all the fun of field trips with Father. But . . . well, to be honest, Fifth Daughter, it was my fault too. I could have studied a bit harder so I'd have been some real use to him, instead of just being a grouch. I mean I can't blame him for wanting to work with Frank — he's a real brain. It's not a bit like, well, like you."

"I *am* glad we are friends. And please do not be afraid. If anything bad should happen you must promise to run back and tell the others — don't wait for me. After all, your legs are much longer than mine."

So she *had* read her thoughts. Valerie's cheeks flamed and she was thankful for the darkness. "No way," she whispered back. "Your legs may be short, but you're much neater and quicker than I am. You run for it, if it comes to that. If they should catch me maybe I could persuade Dr Mushni to take me back."

She felt Fifth Daughter's giggle. "I tell you what, Valerie. If anything should go wrong, let's just stick together."

"Yes, let's." Suddenly Valerie didn't feel half as afraid.

Though it was hard to see the thin line that was the purple road, from up on the ridge where they lay carlights would be visible for a considerable distance. All the time they had been talking they had seen nothing. Both roads were deserted.

"Come on," Fifth Daughter's voice whispered inside Valerie's head. She swallowed and rubbed suddenly damp hands against the thighs of her blue jumpsuit. Fifth Daughter's stumpy legs waddled rapidly over the ground cover and Valerie picked her way carefully after her, trying to make no noise that might alert the inhabitants of the White Tower.

Right up to the edge of the yellow road tufts of wiry grass grew, and they hid among them. To their right, monstrously tall against the dark sky, rose the tower, as quiet as a gravestone. To their left was the intersection of the two highways. Between the two, in the far right quadrant, the forest pressed forward towards the road, its branches stretching out.

Like hungry hands, Valerie thought. She could feel the forest reaching towards them. She shivered. The trees moved, though she could feel no wind. Was the forest really aware of their presence? Was it waiting for them, each tree passing the news on to its neighbour, until the whole forest crept in a slow persistent movement towards them? Or was she just imagining it all?

She looked quickly at Fifth Daughter.

The pink face was expressionless and she reached out to touch. No fear at all! Only an immense curiosity. It was amazing. But then, Fifth Daughter had not seen the place where Frank and the car had been, nor had she felt turf climbing over her feet...

"Once we have crossed the road I will go a little way among the trees. Stay close to the road, Valerie, and keep a look out for cars."

Thank goodness that was all Fifth Daughter wanted her to do. And it was a necessary job after all. She managed a smile. "Good luck."

"You're not afraid?"

"Course not."

"Liar!" She felt a loving wave of warmth like a hug. Then Fifth Daughter nodded and, bent low, they scurried across the yellow road. The soft green turf on the far side seemed welcoming in contrast to the wiry scrub and dry grass. If she hadn't known what it was she would have been happy to lie in it while she watched out for alien traffic. But as it was, her body shrank from contact.

Fifth Daughter darted past her and plunged unhesitatingly into the darkness. Valerie could see the faint glimmer of her pale body among the shadows of the trees.

Don't go, she wanted to cry out, but managed not to. She knelt awkwardly on the grass, hoping she wouldn't be noticeable from the Tower. She couldn't bring herself to lie on that too inviting turf. She looked up and down both roads. They were deserted. All was well.

The grass moved softly, tickling her hands and ankles. She shivered again and rubbed them. The movement stopped, but a moment later the slow tentative stroking began again. She looked down. The grass was moving gently to and fro, like the tentacles of some marine creature. She moved her knees hard across the grass, wanting to hurt it. "Stop that," she whispered angrily. The grass became still.

What was taking Fifth Daughter so long? Was she still there? She stared among the shadowy trees and sudden fear lurched in her tomach. Then she saw her and waved, but the pale blur did not move.

The tickling began again, each blade of grass brushing against her hands, her ankles. She jumped to her feet. There were curved depressions in the grass where she had been kneeling and the grass roots had parted to show the red earth beneath. Like mouths opening. She leapt for the plastic surface of the road. There was nobody to see her, and it didn't matter if they did. She wasn't staying in that spooky forest another second. She walked up the road and down again. To the corner and back. Keep moving, and keep off the grass: that was the way to be safe.

She stopped suddenly. Fifth Daughter wasn't moving. She hadn't moved since she had slipped in among the trees. Surely she should have found out by now whatever she could. *Was* the forest a thinking entity? Or was it just a programmed stomach, like the Venus Flytrap back on old Earth?

She stepped back onto the turf. The grass caressed her ankles and the trees moved to and fro in response to that unfelt wind. She licked her lips. "Fifth Daughter? Please come out. Come out *now*!"

There was no answer and she beat her way between the trees, hitting out at the leafy branches that reached down to stroke her face. There was Fifth Daughter, slumped against a grey tree trunk, her right arm extended, as if she were hugging the tree. And over the fat pink fingers the bark of the tree was slowly growing.

"No!" She pulled at Fifth Daughter. "Wake up. Come away. Oh, can't you feel it? It's eating you up!"

As she shook the humanoid, her fear left her and her hands dropped to her side. But then the terror was back and she dragged at Fifth Daughter's body, forcing her way into the other's mind, trying to overcome the feeling of warmth and friendship that seemed to flow from her like warm syrup.

Fifth Daughter suddenly became aware of Valerie's terror. She pulled her hand away from the engulfing tree. It was lucky, thought Valerie with a shudder, that she was made of soft elastic stuff, instead of being bony like a human. As the pink substance of Fifth Daughter was released with a 'pop' like chewing gum, the bark crept back over the hole where her hand had been. In just a few seconds the surface of the tree was once more smooth and unbroken.

"Oh, come away, please, come away," Valerie pleaded, pulling at Fifth Daughter's arm.

They ran between the sighing trees to the yellow road and were just about to cross when Valerie caught a flash of light in the corner of her right eye. She drew back into the shadows, pulling Fifth Daughter with her.

A car swerved fast around the corner, shot past them along the yellow road and turned into the driveway that circled the White Tower. They heard the furious honking of its horn, a frightened, almost panicky sound. Then an oblong of light appeared in the wall of the Tower. It heightened into a square. The car lurched forward with a sudden clatter of its treads and disappeared into the Tower. They had a second's glimpse of three, maybe four stumpy popeyes. Then the square shrank to an oblong, a slit. To nothing.

"Ah! We've found more than we came for. How pleased they will all be with us. Let's cross before he comes out again."

Fifth Daughter's thoughts were as cheerful as if she was unaware of the horrible fate that had so nearly overtaken her. She stepped onto the road and Valerie tried to follow her. But it was as if her feet were glued to the ground, in that helpless way that happens in dreams.

She looked down and saw, by the faint starlight, the sheen of her blue jumpsuit, thighs, knees, ankles. And no feet. The ground had opened up to swallow her feet. She could feel the grass stroking eagerly at her ankles and opened her mouth to scream.

Fifth Daughter turned as she swallowed the scream and tried to kick her way free. "It's all right. Don't be afraid," the soothing thought came to her. And then Fifth Daughter's spongy hand, surprisingly strong, was in hers and she was pulled free.

Shaking with fear and horror Valerie clung to Fifth Daughter as they ran silently across the road beneath the tall tower and climbed the slope of wiry grass and scrub on the other side.

"Let's wait here and see what happens," Fifth Daughter tactfully suggested, once they were over the crest of the hill and out of sight. Valerie sank down in the scrub, thankful for the chance to pull herself together before the others saw her.

We're quite safe, she told herself firmly. Neither of us was eaten, and the popeyes didn't see us. Fifth Daughter's pleased and it's all right.

"It really is, you know, Valerie. Oh, look. Something's happening."

They couldn't see the door open, since it was on the far side of the Tower, but they saw the glow of light reflected off the yellow road and the trees beyond. There was the sound of an engine revving up. Then the door must have slid shut and there were just two rods of light wavering on the road as the car turned, shot down the yellow road, skidded around the corner and disappeared at top speed down the purple road towards the city.

Valerie could almost see the driver, crouched over the wheel, desperate to get away. What was he afraid of? Not the Tower, obviously. The forest? The driver of the truck she and Isnek had seen before had been terrified too.

"Why, they're as scared of the forest as we are."

"Yes, indeed."

"But that's crazy. It's theirs, after all."

"Oh, no it's not." Fifth Daughter's answer was triumphant inside Valerie's head.

"So you see the forest doesn't belong to this planet either," Valerie told the others as soon as they got back to camp. "It's as alien as we are!"

"How can she possibly know?" Tenkle was sceptical.

"Because the forest told her so. Oh, not deliberately, of course. Do listen." Valerie raised her voice above a babble of protests. "Please, it's terribly important. The whole forest, trees and turf and all, is a single entity. It thinks of itself as 'Moab', and I can't begin to tell you where it's from, but it must be a pretty weird place, from the ideas I get from Fifth Daughter."

"How can a forest be a single entity? The trees, the grass, the soil itself must be part of it, if so. It's ridiculous."

"Not really. It's like something I studied in Alien Biology last year and I remember exactly. It comes from Earth and it's called Portuguese Man-of-War. It floats on top of the sea with a kind of bladder filled with gas, and it has tentacles hanging down as much as thirty metres into the water. They reach out and grab passing fish and put them in its stomach. It even has poisonous cells on the tentacles to paralyse big fish."

"That doesn't sound too unusual."

"The point is it isn't a single organism at all. It's a colony, all making up the entity 'Portuguese Man-of-War'. Each of the parts is an individual, with its own job to do, like the stinging cells, the tentacles, the bladder. All separate, but one — like the forest. Like Moab. Only Moab is much more highly developed."

"All right, Valerie, you're making sense." Tenkle looked at her with a new respect. "But telepathy? That's pretty hard to swallow."

"I don't see why. It would be a convenient way for an entity made up of different kinds of organisms to manage, wouldn't it?"

Doil agreed. "All right, Valerie. Go on."

"The point is that Moab came into the Tower the same way we did. Only the popeyes operating the Transmitter weren't aware of him, because he was only a spore, waiting for the right season to start growing again. He was probably clinging to the fur of some animal captured by the transmitter. That's not very clear."

"When did all this happen?"

"I don't know. Ages ago, I expect. Fifth Daughter was just listening in, you know. I mean, she couldn't ask questions when things weren't clear. Anyway Moab grew into a forest again, trying to reach the Tower. But the road stopped him. He can't transform that plastic stuff into himself the way he could the earth and scrub, so he's been a prisoner at the crossroads ever since."

"Well, it's interesting to know that Moab is in the same boat that we are, but having a carnivorous forest on our side doesn't strike me as much of an asset."

"We don't know that," Valerie said abruptly. She could feel Fifth Daughter's disappointment at the others' lack of interest and she got angry. Being angry seemed to make her brain work. She blushed but went on, "What I mean is that people once tamed the most unlikely animals to be useful. Maybe we can tame Moab."

"Or at least use its natural drive to get to the Tower to our advantage. Val, you've got something here." Frank slapped her back. "After all it's the same drive as ours, isn't it? If we can find a way of using Moab…"

"Especially since the popeyes seem terrified of it." Doil smiled. "The Institute scientists must realise that Moab could over-run the planet if it chose."

"I'm amazed they haven't tried to destroy it."

"Oh, but they have," Valerie spoke for Fifth Daughter. "They tried digging it up and plant killer. Now Moab swallows everything that comes near it. We were dead wrong about it being carnivorous. It's just protecting itself."

"But you'd be just as dead. We've got to be careful."

"Of course. But if we can think of a way of helping Moab cross the road, then we can use it to besiege the Tower, can't we?" Valerie looked from face to face.

There was a moment's silence while they took it in. Then there was a yell from Tenkle and he whirled the sober Doil around in a mad dance. Pretty soon they were all dancing, hugging each other, their voices rising excitedly until one of them would remember how close they were to the enemy and they would quieten down.

Home! Whether it was Persis or Japonica, Tabara or Eden, whatever the name and the memories, in Intergalactic it was the same word for them all. Home!

Back to Mother and Father, thought Valerie rapturously. Back to dull old DeePeeThree. And I don't care a bit. I swear I'll never complain again, even if I have to babysit for ever...

"Oh, Frank," she gasped. "We can't go. Not till we've found Susan. For a moment I almost forgot."

"Me, too. How awful. Look..." He turned to the others. "We'll try and help you find a way to get Moab across the road to the Tower. Once you've escaped you can tell the Federation Police about this place. They'll find us."

Valerie nodded. "Yes, you must go. The police will find us soon enough once you've told them. After all there can't be that many binary systems with livable planets."

"Fourteen hundred and fifty eight at the last census," said Doil crisply.

"That many?" Valerie swallowed. How long would it take before they were rescued? "Well, anyway, we can't leave without Susan and that's all there is to it."

In the silence that followed, Fifth Daughter waddled over to Valerie and laid her paw on Valerie's hand. Valerie listened, smiled and sniffed. "Oh, thank you. But you shouldn't really."

Tenkle spoke. "I certainly want to get back to Nakhan more than anything. But I couldn't do my job well, knowing I'd left you here. I'll stay until we can all go."

"My sentiments precisely."

"Ours too."

"Your logic is badly flawed, but I too will abide by the majority decision." All of them turned to stare at Isnek Ansnek. It was as startling to hear a robot express his personal opinions and take for granted his right to a vote as it would be to hear a table talk.

"Thank you, all of you," Frank stammered. "It's a terrific sacrifice. I...well...thanks anyway." He swallowed. "I'd like to suggest that we form two groups, one headed by Doil to plan the siege of the Tower. He'll need you to explain Moab's reactions, Fifth Daughter." She blushed and nodded. "The second group, to plan the rescue of Susan, I'd like to head if no one objects. Then, when we've come up with all the ideas we can, we could get together and brainstorm, pick holes in each other's schemes if necessary. Eventually come up with a couple of good plans."

"All this talking. I want some action." Tenkle strode up and down. "I am no good with words."

"Ideas first. Frank is right." Doil nodded. "But if you're planning to go into the city to get Susan back you're going to need Fifth Daughter, too, to read the popeye minds."

Fifth Daughter got even pinker. Her surge of happiness was so strong that it swept over Valerie and she found herself laughing. Then the others joined in, and before long they were laughing helplessly. All except Isnek Ansnek, who looked at them as if they'd gone mad. His disapproving expression made them laugh even more than before.

"I will do my best to help," Fifth Daughter said at last. "Thank you for wanting me."

Valerie found herself yawning, a real jaw-cracking yawn.

"Off to bed with you, Val. In fact we should all get some sleep. But not for too long. Once the red sun is up we'll be visible to anyone going by. If anyone ever does. It's not like living in the caves. We should really mount a look-out too. In case..." Doil stifled a huge yawn. Around him heads had already dropped to pillows of dried grass. "Well, perhaps that's not necessary." His head swam with the need for sleep. "I'll just rest for a few minutes," he mumbled.

"I will keep watch and waken you when the red sun rises," said Isnek Ansnek.

"Thanks, old fellow. Very good of you. Sorry we laughed. Nothing personal, you understand..." His head fell back. He snored.

"Think nothing of it," said Isnek Ansnek stiffly.

Down the Road

When Isnek Ansnek wakened them the red sun was just showing above the horizon. Though his face was as expressionless as ever, his bearing was more than a little smug as they yawned, blinked awake and realised they had all slept the whole night through.

Tenkle set about making a hot and almost smokeless fire, and the rest of them gathered the fungus-like flowers off the bushes and put them into a homemade pot to boil. They made a dull but filling food, Valerie had discovered, like porridge or potatoes; if she had starved out in the wilds it would have been in the midst of plenty. Meanwhile the humanoid couple, Sturpis and Filio, went downstream and came back with a string of pink-fleshed fish.

"How did you catch them?"

"With the fingers. Learn when very young. Is an art." Sturpis flicked his fingers along the sides of one of the fishes in a quick rhythm and then, so suddenly that she didn't see his clumsy-looking fingers move, he had hooked it through the gills.

After a tremendous breakfast the fire was put out and the remains carefully scattered, just in case some popeye should come wandering by, though so far there had been little traffic on the roads, none on foot and still no sign of any aircraft. Frank, Isnek, Valerie and Tenkle formed a group to work out plans to rescue Susan, while the others brainstormed the taking of the Tower. Fifth Daughter, bursting with happiness, bustled between the two groups as she was needed, dragging Valerie with her as interpreter.

"But this is silly. You can just as well talk to the others."

"Am used to female household. Not accustomed to speak to man before marriage."

"But Mani is in the other group. You can talk to *her*."

Fifth Daughter waved her arms. "Mani is like my mother," was all she would say, but the way she thought it gave Valerie the giggles. Her feelings were so like Valerie's own, particularly when Mother was being particularly Motherish. It was so funny, when you stopped to think about Fifth Daughter looking just like a lump of pink blancmange, that she should have exactly the same kind of problems.

"Oh, very well." She pretended to be cross. "But I think you're being very silly, Fifth Daughter."

"I'm not. I am exceedingly grown-up. And I *will* talk to Mani, so there, but not yet."

After that they got down to serious planning, drawing plans in the dirt, making lists, assigning jobs. After a few hours the two groups came together and presented their ideas to the other group. Then there was a lot more arguing. Tenkle was particularly good at that. The chief problem was that each group felt that its plan should be put into operation first.

"If you do succeed in finding Susan and getting her away there'll be such an uproar that we'll never be able to take over the Tower."

"But if you manage to take over the Tower first the Institute scientists will be warned. After all, they already know that Frank and I have escaped," Valerie objected. "They're bound to take extra care of Susan."

"What a pity I can't split in two like a Japonican *Pet-*

tilo, so that we could carry out both plans at once," giggled Fifth Daughter.

"You know, it's really quite peculiar that there's been no attempt to catch Valerie and me." Frank rubbed his nose. "What happened when the rest of you escaped?"

"They hunted us constantly. We are not the only humans and humanoids to have escaped, you know. It is just that we are the only ones to have remained free."

"They would have caught me many times." Fifth Daughter's pinkness paled. "But I could sense their presence and hide."

"It is odd, Frank, now you mention it. Two of you at once—that's a big investment. Why should they ignore losing you, when they hunted the rest of us? There must be a logical explanation."

"You and your logic, Doil. Words, words!"

"Tenkle, before you go after one of your poachers, don't you make it your business to find out his habits?"

"Of course. That's why I'm the best."

"This is the same. There is something very odd about the popeyes not attempting to look for these two. Before we risk all our lives, we must try and find out what it is."

They talked on as the red sun moved slowly across the sky, and by sunset their plans were complete, except for one vital detail.

"We must have some transport to the city. Even if we walked there—and we'd waste a couple of days walking—we'd never make it back carrying Susan."

"We could steal a car once we get to the city."

"Suppose you can't? You'll be stuck there."

"What else can we do?"

"Wait till the next car comes up to the Tower and capture it?"

"That would warn the popeyes every bit as much as storming the Tower. They probably have regular schedules for their reliefs. If they don't show up or report back the Institute will know something's up."

Frank groaned and put his hands to his head. Doil looked baffled. In the silence Fifth Daughter prodded Valerie.

"Ow, don't, I'm thinking."

"But I have an *idea*."

"All right then." Valerie sighed. Fifth Daughter's telepathy might prove their greatest strength, but her new sense of self-worth seemed to have flown to her head and she was full of ideas, all of them terrible. "All right. Tell me about it."

"Why not the car you and Isnek came in? The one Moab swallowed?"

"Oh, really, that's quite the silliest..." Valerie was getting tired.

"You see, Moab didn't digest it. I told you it only uses organic materials and air to live on."

"You actually mean it could — well — spit it out again?"

"If you could think of a way of making it. I can't tell it to, you see, or appeal to its better feelings or anything."

Valerie told the others Fifth Daughter's idea.

"Hopeless. If she can't communicate with it how can we?"

"Do you suppose..." Valerie hesitated.

"Go on, Val."

"Well, I don't know much biology, but aren't there ways of making an animal do what you want? Without hurting it," she added quickly, because however peculiar it might look, Moab *was* a living entity.

"You mean like electric shock?"

"In this case you need something like an emetic," Frank suggested. "So it'll bring the car back up."

Tenkle roared with laughter, but Doil interrupted him. "I think you two have got it. I wish we knew how clever

Moab is — I mean, is it as bright as an octopus or only as instinctive as an amoeba?"

Valerie asked Fifth Daughter and spent some time trying to explain about octopi and amoebae. "She thinks it's quite bright, and definitely capable of learning."

"That's all we need. Suppose we make the area right above the car quite unpleasant, do you think Moab might get the idea and give it back?"

"What kind of unpleasant?" Valerie asked suspiciously.

"I was thinking of a small fire."

"That's cruel!"

"Oh, Val, you softy!"

"It'll never work anyway."

They all talked at once until Doil held up his hands for silence. "Whoa, everyone. There's only one way of proving it. Do you think it's worth a try?" They nodded, some doubtfully, some definitely. "All right then. Isnek, can you remember the precise spot where you parked the car?"

"Certainly. I never forget anything."

"No offence. Tenkle, Frank and I will go with Isnek. The rest of you stay in hiding close to the Tower in case anything goes wrong."

"Let me go too," pleaded Valerie. She wasn't going to let Frank out of her sight again. To deliberately irritate Moab sounded horribly dangerous. Suppose the whole glade opened up and swallowed them *all*. She shivered. "I'm coming too, Frank, and that's that!"

"I suppose you could stay by the road and keep look-out." She opened her mouth to protest, but Frank just grinned. "You know very well you'll just get upset if you see us lighting fires. Remember that time Berry got a thorn in his foot?"

Berry was the Eden equivalent of a pet dog. "All right," she said reluctantly. "But you've got to promise to be careful."

"If you remember," Isnek Ansnek swivelled his blank gold eyes towards her, "I told you once before that my own safety is my prime directive. I will make sure that nothing happens to me. Secondly, I will ensure that nothing happens to these others. Does that satisfy you?"

"Yes, thank you, Mr Ansnek."

"Not at all. Now shall we proceed to retrieve the vehicle in question?"

Crossing the yellow road in broad daylight was a very different matter from slipping across in the twilight, and they risked cutting across the corner of the forest that lay between them and the purple road, until they were out of sight of the White Tower.

Moab was very much awake, touching their ankles with grass, reaching down to heads and shoulders with its branches, brushing their faces with its leaves. By the time they had reached the safety of the plastic road again they were shuddering and jumpy, all except Isnek Ansnek, who stalked along calmly as if his mind was light-years away. Perhaps it was, thought Valerie. What do robots think about when they're not working or talking to people? Some time when she wasn't so busy being terrified she'd ask him.

"There is the place," he said suddenly.

"How can you tell?" Frank looked doubtfully at the waving branches.

"Trust me," said Isnek simply.

"All right then." Doil swung the load from his shoulder. The others did the same. "We'll leave most of the firewood by the road and take in only enough for the first fire."

"The first?" Valerie stared.

"Moab's not going to learn right off. It'll take a couple of tries."

"Oh, do be careful."

"We will." Frank gave her a parting hug and headed off through the trees after Isnek and Tenkle.

"Keep a good look-out," Doil warned her. "Whistle or yell if you see a car on the road. And don't be alarmed at Moab's reactions. We'll run back to the safety of the road just as soon as the fire's lit."

Valerie squatted at the edge of the road. It was still, not so much as an insect about, though she could see birds high in the sky above her, little dots soaring in the morning thermals. The purple road stretched like a ruler to left and right. Across the road from the forest the scrub quivered in the breeze.

She turned back to the forest and saw between the trees a thread of smoke. Footsteps thudded across the turf and a few seconds later Frank, Doil, Tenkle and Isnek burst breathlessly out of the trees. Actually Isnek moved rapidly, but gave the impression of strolling.

"What happened?"

"Don't know yet. It's a good hot fire and the turf was really heaving around when we left."

"Poor..." Valerie stopped herself, caught Frank's eye and blushed. They both grinned.

"The smoke is no longer visible," Isnek pointed out.

"Back we go with another load of firewood then."

"Do take care. Moab's going to get awfully mad."

"We will. Don't *worry*, Val."

"I think Moab's going to learn," Doil reported as they came back the second time. "The fire didn't go out. Moab swallowed it."

He was right. As they ran back from lighting the third fire over the place where the car had been the trees rocked to and fro and Valerie saw the men stagger as if they were on a storm-tossed ship. "Phew, that was something," Frank gasped, as he collapsed on the solid surface of the road.

After five minutes the violent rocking died away and cautiously men and robot moved off between the trees to see what had happened.

"Me too!" Valerie ran after them.

She caught up with them at the edge of the glade. There was the car, all in one piece, some clods of soil still on the bonnet and a pile of charred sticks in the middle of the back seat. Isnek Ansnek's memory had been perfect.

"Of course we don't know if it'll even go," Doil warned, as Frank and Tenkle climbed on the high running boards.

But luck was with them. It started the third time Isnek pressed the ignition button, and with all of them aboard it lurched slowly between the trees and out into the sunshine.

"I have the distinct feeling that Moab is saying 'Good riddance'," Frank chuckled.

"Really a car couldn't have been good for its insides."

Isnek drove across the road and about two hundred metres into the scrub. They all piled out and set about sawing at the wiry roots of the dry brush with their homemade knives to make a camouflage cover for the truck. From the road it looked very good.

"Unless a popeye happens to remember that there isn't a hillock just there."

"Which is jolly unlikely. They drove with their heads down at top speed both times I saw them," Valerie reminded Frank.

They kept away from the forest and returned to the Tower through the scrub on the right side of the road, to be met by the others. Fifth Daughter rushed over to Valerie and hugged her.

"What's the matter? Everything went off perfectly."

"Are you all well? No one hurt?"

"Why no." Valerie stared.

"She felt much pain," Turpis grunted and his wife nodded and patted where Fifth Daughter's shoulder would have been if she had had shoulders.

"How silly. I thought one of you must have been hurt. No, there is nothing to fuss about. I am quite fine, I promise you."

After they returned to their temporary camp they grabbed some food and at once Mani set them to collecting grass and spinning it into cord. She tried to teach them all how to knot the cord into mats, but only Fifth Daughter and Tenkle and Isnek Ansnek were able to pick up the skill rapidly enough to be useful. So the others harvested mounds of dry stuff and spun metres and metres of cord until their hands were sore, while the four experts knotted until they had five mats, each about three metres wide, and long enough to reach across the plastic surface of the yellow road and around the driveway to the Tower when placed end to end. Rolled into cylinders the mats could each be carried by two people.

By now the red sun had set and the customary moonless night had fallen over the surface of the alien planet. As quietly as possible they left their camp and climbed to the ridge that overlooked the Tower. All was still. In a single line, each pair carrying a mat between them, they crept down the further slope and across the open space to the Tower.

The mats, dropped among the scrub, blended perfectly with the grass from which they had been made. Here they said goodbye. Only Frank, Valerie, Tenkle, Fifth Daughter and Isnek Ansnek were to make the attempt to rescue Susan. Doil and the two hairy humanoids had agreed that she must be saved before they besieged the Tower. Everyone had volunteered. But Doil had argued that it was foolish to risk them all. A good plan rather than numbers was the key to success.

Frank and Tenkle were the muscle, if it should come to a fight. Valerie was the only one who could read and understand Popeye, and Fifth Daughter was to act as a telepathic look-out. Isnek, of course, could handle the car and open any locked doors that might get in the way.

After hugs and handshakes they slipped past the Tower and across the road to where they had hidden the car. It was a good camouflage job. If Isnek had not been with them they would never have found it in the twilight. It started first go, the engine horribly noisy in the quiet night.

They returned to the city by the same route Isnek and Valerie had taken after their escape from the Zoo, taking the yellow road to their right and the next purple to their left. They passed nothing, but to be on the safe side they drove well past the Zoo before pulling off the road, just in case the guards should hear the car or see the lights.

Keeping to the brush, ready to drop at a sound, they walked back towards the wall that surrounded the Zoo grounds. They heard nothing the whole time but the mournful baying of a caged night animal and the frustrated spit and snarl of a hunter behind bars.

"Wish we could send them all home," muttered Valerie.

"A praiseworthy suggestion," Isnek answered. "But I would not care to attempt enticing a wallaroon or a scramaloupe into the White Tower."

Isnek was right as always, but did he have to be so literal? She knew perfectly well that they'd have to leave it up to the Federation Police to tidy things up on this planet if they got safely home. *When* they got safely home, she corrected herself firmly.

Frank and Tenkle boosted Valerie and Fifth Daughter up onto the top of the wall, so they could lie across it with their legs dangling outside. "There's the gate-house, where the guards hang around when they're not patrolling," Valerie whispered. "See, over on the left, next to the main entrance."

"All right. We'll keep an eye on them after you're gone, and set up interference if there's any trouble. Now where's the Admin building? That's where Isnek is sure the records of incoming specimens will be kept, isn't it?"

"Ninety point three eight percent sure," Valerie whispered back and felt rather than saw Frank's answering grin. She lifted herself up cautiously on one elbow and stared into the darkness. "See that sprawly place behind all the big cages? Over to the right, not far from the wall. I think that must be it. I remember wide glass doors and stairs, but no crowds of popeyes going in and out. Dr Mushni didn't take me in there either."

"All right. Go ahead, you three. And for heaven's sake don't take any unnecessary risks. Val, remember that Fifth Daughter can't yell and Isnek would probably think it beneath his dignity as a free robot, so if anything goes wrong it'll be up to you to let us know, loud and clear. Got that?" He squeezed her shoulder. She could feel the comforting warmth through the too large coverall that she had again donned as a disguise: though of course nothing could disguise the fact that none of them had pop eyes, nor weighed a hundred and fifty kilograms.

She wriggled carefully round and let her legs dangle on the inside of the wall. It was a long way down. Her feet scrabbled for niches in the smooth surface.

"Sssh. You're kicking up an awful racket. It's not as far as it feels. Just relax." Frank caught her wrists and swung her away from the wall and let go. She landed on her feet on the soft ground between the bushes. Without hesitation Fifth Daughter rolled off the wall, bouncing a little as she landed. Well, she's used to a high-gravity planet, Valerie told herself, trying not to feel clumsy and ineffectual.

Though he didn't mean to, sometimes Frank made her feel like an idiot. She started when Isnek Ansnek appeared silently beside her. He looked like the Invisible Man, all black, with only his yellow eyes glowing in the dark.

They set off, staying as close to the wall as they could, always keeping a screen of bushes between them and the nearest path, until they reached the back of the Admin building.

"There'll be a door here," Isnek guessed, and sure enough there was. "Don't touch anything until I've scanned it," he warned them. "As I thought. Alarm wires to the gatehouse. Very amateur stuff. One moment please. There. Now we may enter."

"Fifth Daughter, can you tell if it's empty?"

"I detect no activity, Valerie."

The door let them into a passage with rooms to either side that were obviously offices and storage rooms. At the end of the passage was a wide reception area almost the width of the glassed front.

"Oh my goodness, where am I going to begin?" Valerie looked around in despair at the mountainous filing cabinets that lined the walls of the main office. "I can't read fast enough to get through this lot. Not if we had a week instead of a night."

Fifth Daughter put a pink paw on Valerie's arm. "Tell me exactly what you're looking for."

"Some kind of register, either a book or a file, of all the creatures the transmitter has brought in, and whether they went to the Zoo or the Institute or to a private owner. Something like that. You mean you can help? But you can't read Popeye."

"Often I can tell the feelings that remain on something written. Not always. It depends." She ran a hand down one of the filing cabinets, opening the drawers nd riffling quickly through the files. "This is all to do with personnel.

Salaries, things like that. This one...I wonder. This is about the animals in the Zoo, the history of their upkeep, their medical records, that sort of thing. What else?" She wandered around the room, touching and putting down. "Are you sure what you want will be at the Zoo?"

"No, not really. But the trucks going to the Tower had the Zoo emblem, and so did those thornbushes back on DeePeeThree."

"Hmm. What about this?" She put her pink hand on a black log book that lay conspicuously in the middle of the desk.

Valerie sat in the enormous chair and pulled the book across the desk. She flattened down a page and stared.

"Well?"

"I don't know. It looks..." The ledger was set up in columns. The first Valerie recognised as a set of numbers. Dates, perhaps? The second column was filled with words that were quite unfamiliar to her. The third was more promising. She recognised the character for 'Zoo' and the one for 'Institute'. Others she wasn't sure of. The fourth column had more writing than the others, small to fit into the limited space, and sometimes in a different hand, a different kind of ink. Remarks, perhaps? Added by other people later.

"Is it the right one? Is it?"

"I think so."

"We have not much time, Valerie."

"I can't hurry." She turned the pages feverishly. Wasn't that Dr Mushni's name? She puzzled out the scrawl in the remarks column. Subject to...to educational lab for research purposes.

Why, that was *her*!

"Valerie, the guards are patrolling. They are not far from this building. I can hear their thought patterns."

Valerie shut the book. "Let's go. We'll work out what this means in the car."

"Won't they miss it?"

"Surely not tonight. Who cares if they miss it in the morning? With any sort of luck we'll have Susan and be gone by then. Come on."

They slipped like shadows out of the back door, Isnek Ansnek stopping to lock it behind them. As they edged their way along the wall behind the shrubs they could see the occasional flash of light, hear the voices of the two guards, extraordinarily loud on the still night air. They crouched by the wall until the popeyes had gone into the Admin Building, and then with the help of Frank and Tenkle they scrambled back over the wall. They had regained the car before a distant flash of light told them that the guards were back at the gatehouse.

They drove a little further into the bushes and Isnek turned on a light above the dashboard. Valerie flattened the book open at the page that held the entry with Dr Mushni's name and held it close to the light. There were a lot of entries for that particular day. The popeyes had been busy. On some days there were no entries at all. On others only one or two. Why? Something to ask Doil when they got back.

Her entry was the last on that particular day. She remembered that hers had been the last in the line of cages at the market place. Next to her had been the wallaroon, destined for the Zoo, she knew, since she had seen it there. Her finger moved to the third column. Yes, there was the sign for 'Zoo'.

Beyond the wallaroon had been Isnek Ansnek. She looked at the third column. There again was the symbol for the Institute and Dr Mushni's name. She puzzled over the 'remarks' column, but could make nothing of it at all.

Further up the page, still under the same date, there was an entry that contained the symbol 'Two' in the second column. Two specimens, her mind jumped. Surely that was it. Frank and Susan! She took a shaky breath.

One of the pair had the 'Zoo' designation. The other...
the other had an unfamiliar name and a private address.
She puzzled out the symbols. Then... "I've got it! The
widow Karosh, 23 Ninth Avenue." She slammed the book
shut and looked triumphantly at the others.

"Good for you, Val. Now how in the world do we find it
without a map? We can hardly stop to ask for directions."

"23 Ninth Avenue," Tenkle repeated. "That shouldn't
be too hard. Avenues one direction, streets the other."

"Yellow and purple. If we just knew which was which."

"But I do, Frank. How silly! The ideogram for 'yellow'
is almost the same as that for 'avenue'. It's like a pun. So
it's the ninth yellow road. Only counting from where?
From this side of town? From the middle?"

"We're going to look awfully conspicuous driving right
through town counting avenues, but I suppose it's the only
way."

"We can stay on this street as long as possible, Frank. It
seems to be right out in the suburbs. Oh, maybe we'll get
lucky."

And lucky they got. As they drove down the purple road
they came to a place where repairs were being done,
though what could go wrong with a plastic road they
couldn't guess. Perhaps it had something to do with drains.
Anyway, there was a heap of equipment and a sign, that
said clearly enough for Valerie to read: "Detour via Ninth
Avenue." An arrow even pointed the way.

Ninth Avenue was the third yellow road after the sign.
They turned left along it, into a suburban neighbourhood
of houses set far apart in extensive grounds.

"It looks very grand."

"I suppose only the very rich can afford pets from other
planets. It's probably a kind of status symbol," Valerie
guessed. She shivered. They were so close to finding Susan.
"Oh, don't let anything go wrong now," she prayed.

Some of the houses had fancy names on signs above the gates, the Popeye equivalent, Valerie supposed, of 'Dunroamin' and 'Innisfree'. But the twelfth house on the left had a number, clearly painted above the ironwrought gate. 'Twenty-three'.

"Bingo!" said Frank softly.

"Are we going to drive right in?" Valerie whispered. "There's no cover out here."

"I think so. It's an awfully long driveway. I'll feel more comfortable with our escape route close to the action."

"The gravel on the drive will announce our arrival somewhat conspicuously," Isnek put in.

"That's why we're going to drive across the lawn and park on the opposite side of the house to those garage buildings." Frank pointed.

"On the grass!" Isnek stared. "But roads are for . . . yes, I see. What a good idea."

He drove the car bumpily over a wide expanse of lawn and parked it under a grove of cabbage trees to the left of the house. Frank jumped down to the ground and gave Valerie and Fifth Daughter a hand.

"All right. You all know what to do. Tenkle and Isnek check the grounds. Fifth Daughter tells us what's going on in the house. Come on, Val, time we found our Susan."

Fifth Daughter moved quietly away, and by the time Valerie and Frank had reached the house she was waiting for them.

"One small person asleep. Brain waves similar to yours, Valerie. Also two popeyes, both awake. I think they play cards. It is hard to read their thoughts as they are concentrating, but they are anxious and irritable. Perhaps their game is not going well. One is male and one female. That is all I can tell."

"Mr and Mrs. Or maybe not. Well, we all know what to do. Are you ready, Valerie?"

"Susan is in the small room at the back of the house. Fifth Daughter thinks it is a...a pantry. The window is open."

"Almost too easy," quipped Frank. "You'd think the widow Karosh would be more careful with her valuable pet."

"Oh, Frank, don't. Come on. I can't wait another minute."

They found the open window without difficulty and Frank gave Valerie a boost onto his shoulders. She pushed the window up carefully, holding her breath, but it moved quietly and easily. She slid into the darkness within and tried to get her bearings. It was little bigger than a very large cupboard, with shelves along two walls filled with enormous tins of popeye food. On the floor was a large basket, and in it, under a blanket that had seen better days, was Susan.

Valerie had to bite her lip to stop herself from crying. There had been so many black days when she had thought she would never see her little sister again. And here at last... She knelt down by the basket, pushing a feeding dish out of the way, and put one hand over Susan's mouth.

"Susan love, wake up," she whispered. "It's Val. I've come to take you home."

"I think not, Vally," an odiously familiar voice spoke from the darkness by the door. Then the overhead light glared on.

Moab Makes a Move

"What a lot of trouble you have given me, Vally. After my kindness to you it is too bad."

Susan wakened with a frightened wail, and Valerie caught her up in her arms and held her close, staring at Dr Mushni defiantly above her head. "I'm surprised to see you again, Dr Mushni," she lied.

"Foolish child. Did you not think that after your disappearance and that of the specimen in the Zoo on the same day I would not check back. Three of you arrived from the same planet within a few minutes of each other. Could you be related? So I had a long talk with this little pet..."

He reached out to pat the top of Susan's head. Valerie drew back quickly and Dr Mushni's face turned a deep red and his eyeballs retracted and shot out again.

"I would not have hurt her. I am a scientist, not a savage. It was not easy talking to this one since she did not understand Intergalactic, and my English, in spite of your excellent teaching..." He bowed mockingly to Valerie. "My English is not good. But as soon as I talked about Vally, oh yes, you could see how interested the little pet was. I knew that sooner or later you and your friend—or might it be another sib?—would try to steal this little pet away from its owner. No need to waste time on expensive searches. All I had to do was to wait. I knew you would come. So simple. Were you not surprised at how simple it was to find the log book? To find the correct house?"

Valerie bit her lip. I just won't give him the satisfaction of answering, she told herself firmly. Besides, if I get mad, I might give away too much. She pushed back the tangled fair hair from Susan's face. It was pale and pudgy and the eyes looked huge and black. "She looks just awful," Valerie's voice shook. "What have you been doing to her?"

"Nothing, nothing. The Zoo vet put a little medicine in its food, that is all. It fussed and cried so much that the owner was almost ready to have it put down. But it is much better now, eating very well and getting nice and fat, and she is pleased with it. A very wealthy widow," he said in a lower voice. "And a great patron of the Institute."

Poor Susan. Valerie felt a sob rise in her throat and she swallowed hard and kissed the top of Susan's head. "Well, I'm glad she's been doing well. It was worth the try to rescue her anyway. What happens now?"

"That depends on you, Vally. Professor Hushino is very angry. You remember him? The Head of the Institute. He tested you himself the night before you were so naughty and ran away."

Valerie remembered and shivered. She clenched her hands until the nails dug in. She wouldn't let him see how scared she was at the memory of the giant popeye.

"He wants to eliminate you and have no more trouble for the Institute. But I . . . I have not finished my work. How can I write a paper when the work is incomplete? I *think* that if you were to tell me exactly where I can find the specimen you stole from the Zoo, and if you were to help me get it back with no fuss and no killing—a valuable specimen, after all—then I may be able to persuade Professor Hushino not to terminate you—at least not until my work is finished. Where is the other one, Vally? Is it outside? Call it in now and tell it that the young one is here and that it is safe to come in. Will you do that, Vally? To save your life?"

"I . . . I can't," she stammered, thinking furiously. "You see, we — the two of us — escaped up the purple road from the city. We walked for a very long time and it was night again and we were so tired and there was a forest. We thought it would be a good place . . . to . . . hide . . ." She faltered, looking up under her eyelashes to see Dr Mushni turn pale.

"I woke after a while. There was a noise. Frank was screaming. The forest was swallowing us up. The turf was over my ankles. It was horrible, disgusting. I kicked my legs free and tried to help Frank, but it was too late. He was in too deep. So I ran. It was a terrible place." Now at last it was all right to cry and she let the tears flow thankfully.

"Yes, yes." Dr Mushni nodded, his eyes retracted right into his head. "Is a bad place." Then his eyes shot out again, glaring at her. "How you manage to live?"

"Huh? Oh, you mean food? There were things like flowers that were eatable. And plenty of fresh water."

"Then you suddenly decide to return for your sib, just like that?"

"Yes." Don't explain, Val, she told herself. Too many words could get you into trouble. But Dr Mushni went on staring at her with his eyeballs extended until the silence was unbearable. "I was so lonely. I thought if I could only rescue Susan we could manage to get up into the mountains and live there, pick berries, maybe fish."

"A difficult life for a small one. Selfish of you, was it not, Vally?"

"Better for her than prison."

"How you exaggerate!"

"If one is not free, then life is a prison."

"It is all relative, is it...why, what was that?" Dr Mushni stopped talking and tilted his head. Valerie's heart pounded.

"I heard nothing," she said loudly.

"Hush." He pushed her roughly out of the way and leaned out of the window. "Guards! Guards!"

There was a thump and he suddenly disappeared head first. Valerie held her breath. There was a creak in the passage outside. "Lie in your basket and don't say a word, Susie, love," she whispered. "Don't be scared. Val will look after you."

She sped across the room and flattened herself against the wall behind the closed door.

"Dr Mushni, is everything all right?" A high voice wavered from the other side of the door. It opened slowly. Valerie held her breath. "Oh, I thought you were in..." Valerie threw her whole weight against the open door. It met a large obstacle with a smack. There was a gasp, and Valerie leapt around the door to pounce on the fat mound that lay across the threshold. It was limp and the eyeballs had retracted into the head.

Well done, Val, she told herself. She had seen it done on video, but she didn't know it would work so effectively. She heaved the fat lump over and took a length of grass twine from the front of her coveralls to tie the woman's wrists together. There was enough string left to tie to the door knob. That should hold her for a while.

"It's all right, Susan. The bad man's gone. It's time to go home. Come on." Her arms cracking with the strain, she swung Susan up onto the windowsill and let her down as far as she could before letting her drop to the grass. Then she tidily turned out the light and climbed out after her.

Susan's arms clamped frantically around her neck, choking her. "Let go, Susie love. It's all right. Truly. Hush." Her eyes flicked around and her ears strained. The grounds were quiet and dark. There was no sign of life from the neighbouring houses over there, beyond the groves of cabbage trees. Dr Mushni was nowhere to be seen. Valerie smiled. It was all going according to plan.

She managed to disentangle Susan's arms from round her neck and scrambled to her feet. "Come on. Give me your hand. You're going to meet a special friend of mine, and then we'll all go for a car ride. No, it's all right . . . don't. . ."

Susan pulled her hand away and turned to run at the sight of Fifth Daughter, sitting patiently, round and pink, in the back of the popeye car. Valerie grabbed her and picked her up, struggling and crying. "I don't want to. I don't. . ."

"But she's my friend."

Fifth Daughter bounced down from the back of the car and extended an arm to touch Susan. At once she relaxed and the terror faded from her face. Valerie helped Fifth Daughter lift her up onto the back seat of the car. "Thank goodness for your telepathy. She's far too scared to listen to sense. Fifth Daughter, where are the others? Surely they should be here by now?"

"They took Dr Mushni to that building over there. I think it is a place to store cars."

"But why aren't they back?"

"They are still fighting the Institute guards that Dr Mushni had waiting there."

"Goodness, why didn't you say so at once?" Valerie jumped down from the car. "Take care of Susan, Fifth Daughter."

She ran silently across the manicured lawns towards the big building that lay among lesser outbuildings to the right of the house. The night was still, but as she got closer to the garage she could hear an occasional muffled sound, a grunt, the sound of something hollow falling and rolling before coming to rest.

Wait for me, boys, she thought and tore open the door.

It opened onto a staircase that must lead to an upstairs apartment — for the chauffeur, she guessed. To her right an archway led to the garage where two vehicles were parked. One of them was an expensive-looking car. The other was an Institute van. Above her head something heavy crashed.

She turned, then changed her mind and ran into the garage. When she came back a minute later she had a metal bar like a tyre iron in her hand. Upstairs the lights were blazing, though the shutters had been tightly closed so that no light had shown outside.

In one corner lay Dr Mushni, neatly bound in grass rope. Three large popeyes were fighting with Frank and Tenkle. As she stood in the entrance Tenkle's huge muscles bulged and a popeye flew across the room towards her. Before he could get to his feet, Valerie shut her eyes and whacked him with the tyre iron. With only one opponent Tenkle seemed to be in control, so she ran across the room to help Frank, who was half the weight of his adversary, besides being in poor condition after all those weeks of Zoo slops.

The popeye was trying to climb onto Frank's back. Frank's bad knee gave and he fell with the popeye sprawled on top of him. Valerie swung again with her tyre iron. This time she had to keep her eyes open for fear of hitting Frank.

Behind her Tenkle's opponent collapsed with a thump.

"Good girl," Frank gasped as he crawled out from under the weight of the popeye. "Give me your rope, will you?"

"I used all mine on the widow what's-her-name."

"Perhaps this will do." Isnek Ansnek emerged from the bedroom. He was busy tearing a sheet into strips with strong metal fingers.

"Thanks." Frank tied up his popeye and went to help Tenkle.

"Where were you when we needed you?" Tenkle challenged Isnek. He was breathing hard and a cut on his right cheekbone was bleeding sluggishly.

"I am not constructed for fighting. It seemed appropriate to wait unseen for the outcome."

"Hmmm. Val's not constructed for fighting either and she did a slap up job."

Valerie blushed. "It was my trusty tyre iron — or whatever it is. I hope they're not hurt too badly, are they?"

"Not to worry, Val. They'll have rotten headaches when they wake up, that's all."

"Everything secure here. Let's go. It must be nearly dawn."

The white sun shone like a nova as they clattered out of the garage. "Not much time," Tenkle grunted.

"Hang on. We should disable the cars." Frank slid to a stop.

"Done," panted Valerie. "Before I came up. Let's go."

They raced across the grass to the car. "Susie! Oh, thank God you're safe." Frank's voice broke. He jumped up into the back, but Susan shrank back against Fifth Daughter's side and began to cry.

"Go away. You're awful and I hate you, Frank Spencer. I want my Valerie."

"But, Susie..."

"Come on. No time for that now." Tenkle pulled Frank down from the running board and pushed him in front next to Isnek. Valerie climbed up onto the back seat and felt Susan's arms go round her. Just for a minute she felt a surge of pure triumph. Susan loved *her* more than Frank. He was no longer the do-nothing-wrong, the favourite. Red with shame she pushed the rotten thought out of her head. Something's wrong between Susan and Frank. Something I'm going to have to sort out and put right. But not now. There isn't time now...

The engine turned over sweetly, and Isnek expertly turned the car and steered across the grass to the front gates. Then, instead of turning right towards the safety of the quiet countryside, he swung the car to the left.

"Hey, stop!"

"Have your circuits fused, Isnek?"

"Mr Ansnek, stop! This way goes right through town."

In spite of their shouts Isnek drove on imperturbably. "It has occurred to me that since we were expected at the Zoo and at the widow's house, there is a ninety-nine point eight percent probability that there will be a road block awaiting us. Where the sign was, I should surmise. I hope to outwit them by taking a different route."

"Phew! You're right, of course. We should have thought of that."

"Good old Isnek. Hang on, everyone. He's driving this thing like a rocket." The car skidded and they fishtailed madly.

"I am an exceedingly good driver." Isnek struggled to straighten the car. "But these roads are inferior to the main highways. I shall take care."

They hurtled through the sleeping suburbs into a more built-up area. Isnek ignored several side roads and turned up a purple road wider than the others. "We must hope I have made the right choice. I am eighty-eight point six percent sure, but I would be happier with a higher degree of certainty."

"You're doing fine, Isnek. Just concentrate on driving and don't talk, there's a good chap."

The houses were closer together. They became interspersed with what seemed to be shops and public buildings. Without warning the purple road vanished and they were in the familiar market place with its squares of purple and yellow paving. Isnek ran straight across the middle and out the far side.

"This is it," gasped Valerie between bounces. "This is the way the truck brought me in."

"Right on, Isnek. Good for you."

"So far. There is a remote possibility that there is a road block at the next crossroads. It depends on how thorough they are."

"Dr Mushni was only using Institute staff." Valerie put in. "Ouch! I think they didn't want to let anyone else know how careless they were."

The red sun bounced above the horizon like a bright beach ball as they reached the next major yellow inter-section. It was deserted, but as they sped by Valerie looked anxiously to their left. Far in the distance she could see two cars.

"Oh, quickly, Mr Ansnek."

"We are proceeding as fast as this vehicle will permit."

They climbed into the foothills. "But something's wrong. We should be seeing the forest on our left by now."

"Look ahead. Something's happened to the highway. Are you *sure* we're on the right road?"

Isnek coasted to a halt. Ahead of them the straight purple ribbon of road came to a sudden end in a thick tangle of alien trees.

"It's Moab. He's gone and spread across the purple road."

"But *this* wasn't the plan. We'll have to leave the car and go the rest of the way on foot. Come on!"

They ran forward into the forest where the trees closed around them, shutting out the morning sunlight.

"At least the popeyes won't dare follow us in here," gasped Valerie.

"I'm not so keen on it myself," Frank replied with a humourless grin. "I hope it doesn't know that we're the ones that lit those fires in it. Can you go a bit faster?"

"Not with Susan."

"Give her to me."

But Susan refused to look at Frank and screamed with anger when he tried to touch her. Valerie staggered on with Susan riding piggy back and at length they found themselves at the base of the White Tower, changed out of all recognition with turf growing up to its walls and trees crowding close. A vine had put out a feeler. As Valerie watched, it crept up the smooth wall and reached out towards one of the high narrow windows.

A tickling around her ankles warned Valerie not to linger. She hitched Susan up, took a deep breath and followed the others. Behind the Tower the trees soon thinned and it was not long before she burst out into sunshine again. The struggle over the last ridge was almost more than she could manage, but there were Mani and the two humanoids Sturpis and Filio. Doil was tending a small fire and there was the wonderful smell of fresh fish grilling.

"Oh, it's so good to see you all again." She swung Susan down to the ground and impulsively hugged Mani and the two hairy humanoids.

Frank turned to Susan, who was standing with her thumb in her mouth staring at Sturpis and Filio and looking as if she might start crying again. "Come on, little sister, meet the gang."

She backed away from him.

"Hey, what *is* all this?"

"I hate you. You're so mean." She did begin to cry in earnest. Frank's face turned red.

Valerie dropped to the ground and took her sister on her lap. "Now what's all this nonsense? Tell Val."

The words came hesitatingly at first, and then in a rush. "He didn't want to babysit me. He took me in the maze place and left me there and then I was *here* in a cage with those awful things and I had a headache and I was sick and I called and called him but he didn't come."

"Now you just listen, Susie. Frank didn't leave you. You and he were caught in the Space Trap together. It wasn't his fault. Once you got here they put you to sleep and then put you in separate cages."

"But I called and called and nobody came." It was a cry of absolute despair, and Valerie realised that Susan's life on this planet had given her deep wounds that couldn't be healed by just a few words. It would take the doctors back on Eden to make everything right again. But she could at least try, for Frank's sake as well as Susan's.

"That's because Frank stayed asleep longer than you did. He just didn't hear you. And after you went to stay with the fat woman he was put in..." She couldn't say the Zoo, it was too demeaning. "Put in a kind of prison. He just couldn't get out and help you, however much he wanted to."

"But *you* came and got me." Susan's head butted Valerie's chest.

"I just fell through the Space Trap by mistake." Valerie swallowed and went on bravely. "You've got to understand, love. I would never in a million years have been brave enough to come through on purpose, even to get you. It was an accident, and then I got lucky and met Isnek Ansnek and he helped me get Frank, and everyone helped rescue you."

Susan sniffed. "She was so horrible. That fat person. Her eyes waved around and she kept patting and punching me and saying I was too thin. And she got mad at me when I didn't eat the horrible food, and she made me eat it. And then she tried to teach me all sorts of stupid things, like running after a ball, just as if I was a baby."

Valerie hid a smile. "Well, it's over now. We all know you're a big girl, and you're going to have to show us, because we still have to find a way out of this place, and everyone is going to have to help, including you. All right?"

"But I want to go home *now*." Susan's lip trembled.

"Here." Fifth Daughter stretched out her arms to Susan and soon they were sitting together and Valerie could hear, when she touched Fifth Daughter, that she was telling Susan a story. "Once upon a time there was a brave little girl called Susan..."

Frank pulled Valerie to her feet and gave her a hug as fierce as one of Sturpis's.

"What's that for?"

"For being such a great guy. For putting things right between Susan and me. You needn't have..."

"I know. It crossed my mind," Valerie blurted out. "Wasn't that awful of me, Frank? I actually thought for a minute, Susan could be my best friend for life and not like you any more. I'm ashamed of myself."

"Don't be. You've become quite a person since I saw you last, Valerie Spencer."

It was quite ridiculous to feel so happy when they were all prisoners on an alien planet and their escape route had been cut off by a wild alien forest and popeyes were panting up the road behind them...

"Oh, the popeyes! What *are* we going to do?"

"Eat first." Doil handed her a piece of sweet hot fish. "We'll need all our energy to face Moab and get into the Tower."

"What I can't understand is why you changed the plan, Doil," Tenkle said bluntly. "Sunrise was the signal to put the mats across the road so that Moab could cross the plastic."

"That's exactly what we did, my dear Tenkle. It was incredible. The forest just poured across the road and around the Tower like a flood. We had completely misjudged Moab's speed of travel. Or its desire to reach the Tower."

"What now? We were going to drive up to the door as if we were from the Institute. The door would have opened and we'd have driven inside before they'd an idea who we were. Now we're sunk."

"Never trust a vegetable as an ally," Tenkle grumbled. "It was always the weakest part of the plan."

"Can we force our way into the Tower?" Valerie asked and yawned jaw-crackingly.

Doil threw some twigs on the fire. "Rest for a bit. You've had a busy night. Isnek and I will take another look, though I must say *I* couldn't see a way in."

Valerie watched Isnek follow Doil through the trees.

"You're looking very smug," Frank said in her ear.

She blushed. "I was just thinking how well he was functioning. Did I tell you I put him together? He grumbled about needing a refit, but I think he looks terrific."

"So do I. Smart girl." He looked at her with his head on one side.

"What is it?"

"You know what a time you've had with biology and geology at school? I was thinking, there's no law says you have to do the same work as Father and Mother and me. Did you ever think about robotics?"

"Oh, what a splendid idea! But that time Mr Ansnek was telling me what to do."

"They'll tell you at tech college, silly. Anyway, it's something to think about, once we're home."

"I will. And thank you, Frank." Not just for the idea, she thought, but for the way he'd said 'once we're home'. As if it was inevitable.

Then Doil and Isnek Ansnek were back.

"No go, I'm afraid. The door mechanism is on the inside, of course, and the join is so precise that there's no way we can jam it or break our way in."

"What about those windows?" Valerie remembered the creeper feeling its way around the window-frame.

Doil shook his head. "Even Moab couldn't get in there. It's hopeless for us."

"Mr Ansnek, when I first put you together again you were ready to escape. *You* must have had a plan?"

"I had several. But none of them included nine humanoids and an over-eager vegetable. I am sorry I can be of no more help at this time. In fact I would estimate our chance of entering the Tower under the present circumstances at..."

"That's all right, Isnek, thanks," said Frank hurriedly.

"You don't know how to get home, do you?" Susan struggled out of Fifth Daughter's arms. "None of you know. We're stuck here and I'm never going to see Mummy and Daddy again!"

"You are." Valerie hugged her. "I promise you are. We're going to find a way, aren't we, Frank?"

She looked up at him, white-faced.

In the silence that followed they all heard popeye voices a long way off, on the other side of the forest called Moab.

10

The Siege of the White Tower

"We've got to think of a way of making the popeyes open the door." It was too cruel to be this close to freedom, Valerie thought. I'd sooner die than be recaptured...But then she looked down at Susan, clinging to her hand. No I wouldn't. Not as long as Susan's here to be looked after.

"Valerie's right," Doil said. "Forcing the door is impossible. Unless we can think of a way of tricking the popeyes into opening it for us, we're done."

"I'd sooner run for it, before they decide to go around the forest and come on us from behind. If we leave now we might make it to the mountains."

"We agree with Tenkle," Sturpis put in, and Filio nodded, clutching his hairy arm.

Valerie looked down at Susan and then stuck her chin up. "I won't run. Susan's too small to keep up with us, and if we carry her it'll hold us back. Anyway it's no life for a little girl. She needs her mother and father." Her voice wobbled, and she swallowed her tears and went on. "I don't want to stay here and be starved out or recaptured either. We're giving up too easily. There's got to be a way."

She was so afraid that she wanted to sit down and cry. If only she was as little as Susan, she could run to someone's arms and they'd look after her. Oh, Mum, she thought. I wish you were here. You'd think of something...

She tried to imagine the kind of advice Mother would give if she *were* here now, and funnily enough an idea popped into her mind, though whether it would have come anyway she had no way of knowing.

"Fifth Daughter, you can feel what people are thinking even when they aren't trying to communicate with you?"

"This is true, though only with strong emotions, like fear or anger."

"Could it work the other way round. I mean, could you send out a signal to someone who wasn't telepathic?"

Fifth Daughter read Valerie's mind and grew pinker, "Oh, yes, especially if they were in a fearful state to begin with. It might be possible to influence the popeyes to open the door for us."

Valerie explained to the others. "If we all held hands and concentrated like mad, like in a seance, you know."

"Ha!" Tenkle jumped to his feet. "We all think: 'Open the door. Open the door'. And they will do it? Is that possible?"

"No, not like that. That's too specific. We've got to send a message at a much more primitive level."

They stared blankly at each other.

"What do most creatures fear the most?" Doil asked.

"Fire," said Tenkle unhesitatingly. "Almost every living creature fears fire. Would it work?"

Valerie consulted Fifth Daughter. "She thinks so. It's worth a try, isn't it? Better than running for the rest of our lives or being recaptured."

"All right. We'll have to get as close to the Tower as possible and hope Moab doesn't get ideas of swallowing us before we've succeeded. All holding hands with Fifth Daughter somewhere in the middle of the line since her mind is the strongest."

"Since I am not capable of generating emotion I am useless in this exercise," said Isnek Ansnek. "I will stand as close to the door as possible, ready to secure the opening if you succeed."

"Good idea."

"What about poor old Moab?" Valerie protested. "It wants to escape too."

"My good girl, you can't put a forest in a matter transmitter, however advanced the design and however good your intentions."

"Valerie's got a point, though," Frank said. "What's to stop Moab from surging into the Tower as soon as the door's open and gumming up the works with branches and creepers?"

"Look at the way it crossed the road," Tenkle added. "Faster than you'd believe possible."

"But we can't transport a tree, much less a forest," said Doil again.

"Mummy and Daddy take seeds to new planets. It's silly to take trees. They're too big," Susan suddenly spoke up.

They all turned to stare at her and her cheeks went pink and she pushed her face against Valerie's waist.

"Well, out of the mouth of babes..." said Doil. "Bless the child, she's got it. *Are* there any seeds?"

Fifth Daughter reached up and picked a cluster of dry wing shapes from a tree at the edge of the forest. She held them out to Valerie.

"No, I want to take them. It was my idea, wasn't it?"

"It certainly was, Susan. And so you shall. Take great care of them. Maybe in your pocket?"

"How do we know Moab will understand?" Frank asked.

"It's a chance we'll have to take, but it seems to me that as soon as the seed is in the Tower the rest of Moab will know it and leave us alone."

"Come on!" Tenkle was impatient. "Let's get started."

They moved through the trees until they came to the smooth white wall of the Tower.

"Link hands, everyone. All right, now think of fire. No, that's not it. *Feel* fire. Feel fear and smoke and heat. Feel choking and not being able to breathe. Feel the need to get out into the fresh air."

They stood as close as they could, facing the Tower, and concentrated. Each of them in their own way reached out to this single primitive fear.

Fire, thought Valerie with one half of her mind. I hate fire. I'll imagine that I'm in a small room with smoke coming in. It's getting hotter and hotter and I'm choking to death. I've got to get out...

The other half of her mind thought: Is it going to work? I can't hear anything. What are the popeyes doing down at the end of the road? I hope Moab doesn't start eating us. I can feel the grass tickling. Oh, dear, it isn't going to work!

She tried to force the two parts of her brain to concentrate on fear, fire; fear, fire.

"This isn't working." She heard Fifth Daughter's voice in her head. "It is not an exercise in meditation. We need raw primitive emotion."

Beyond the forest popeye voices were raised. Someone was shouting orders. Suppose they're coming now, thought Valerie, and felt a twinge of real fear.

Suddenly a shudder ran through the ground. The branches of the trees around them lashed out frantically and the leaves hissed with pain.

Fifth Daughter winced and Valerie felt the pain she suffered. On Valerie's other side Susan screamed and tried to run. Valerie tightened her grip on her hand. "Hang on," she cried to the others. "Don't let go. No one let go!"

"Fire!" Susan's voice was a scream of terror. "I want my Mummy. Take me home. I'm burning up. Oooh!"

A shudder ran down the line. Behind them the trees swayed and moaned.

"Don't fight it." Sweat ran down Valerie's face, salty into her panting mouth. "Let...the...fear...come... in."

Together they shared and passed on the agony that was Moab's. Flamethrowers, Valerie realised. They're using flamethrowers to clear the road. Soon the fire'll spread and the smoke really will choke us. Then flames, awful searing flames...

They swayed to and fro, their hands clinging to each other, Sturpis linked to Filio and she to Frank, Frank to Susan, Susan to Valerie, Valerie to Fifth Daughter and she to Mani, Mani to Tenkle and Tenkle to Doil.

Fire...Flame...Fear...

"The door is opening," Isnek reported in his dry voice.

Nobody heard him.

"THE DOOR IS OPENING"

The trance was broken and they ran for the door, Frank picking up Susan as he ran. They passed four scientists, who ran blindly past them, coughing, choking, pop-eyes watering, stubby four-fingered hands clutching at choking thoats. They ran from the safety of the Tower out into the fury of Moab and the smoke and fire.

Isnek was first inside. He swiftly scanned the instruments, his brain selecting, rejecting. By the time Sturpis, at the end of the line, had gained the safety of the Tower, Isnek was ready to touch the correct button.

The door slid down. Outside the scientists turned, but they were too late. Valerie, Frank and the others saw them run forward, hands outstretched to the closing door. Susan screamed and buried her face in Frank's neck. The door shut with a thunk.

Within the Tower humans and humanoids looked around, dazed. Susan still cried, and Valerie took her from

Frank and mopped up her tears. The solid warmth, the teary face and a request that Val find a bathroom *now* brought her back to reality.

The others also made connections. The hairy humanoids hugged each other like great bears. Doil and Tenkle shook hands and grinned. Frank hugged Valerie and Susan, while Mani, the cool reserved Mani, ran to Fifth Daughter and put her arms around her. "Oh, my poor child, what you must have suffered! Are you all right, my dear?" And Fifth Daughter put her head on the shoulder of the despised Mani and wept.

Ignoring this emotional orgy Isnek Ansnek prowled, absorbed, catalogued, enquired and formulated possibilities. There were tapes on a shelf of the instrument console. He began to examine them.

Slowly the others separated and began to look around. What was this place that held the Space Trap that had brought them here?

The Tower was basically a hollow shell, some ten metres in diameter and about forty metres high. To the right of the entrance door was an instrument console that occupied a quarter of the wall space. Beyond it a spiral staircase wound dizzily up to a mechanism controlling an enormous lens that hung in a network of cables directly below the transparent domed roof.

Beyond the foot of the staircase were a set of doors leading to the living quarters of the staff. The rooms were built out into the Tower, following the curve of its wall and occupying about one half of the wall space. Above the rooms, which were one storey high, was storage space, reached from a platform extended from the spiral staircase.

The whole centre of the Tower was empty, except for a square cage, made of heavy bars, each wall of which was about four metres wide and high. The whole thing was topless and lay directly beneath the dome and the huge lens.

So that's how we arrived, thought Valerie, staring up into the dizzy heights. Still holding Susan's hand she walked around the cage and opened the first door to her left. It opened to a windowless but well-lit room with a kitchen built in on the right, a table and four chairs, and to the left a grouping of armchairs and a bookcase. All of it appeared over-sized and clumsy like all popeye furniture she had seen.

When she turned the tap above the sink fresh water ran freely. She swung open a cupboard door. Food of a sort. Popeye food. They could last out a limited siege anyway, until the popeyes realised they were all inside the Tower and cut off their water supply. The next room was a bathroom with huge basin, lavatory and shower. She left Susan there and went back to the kitchen and lined up all the jugs and pots she could find and filled them with water. When Susan was ready they explored two bedrooms, each furnished with just a built-in bunk and a dresser and shelves. The Tower was certainly going to be a most comfortable place to camp, for as long as they could hold out against the popeyes.

By the time Valerie and Susan had finished their exploration they found the others had gathered around Isnek Ansnek, who was attempting to explain to them the operation of the matter transmitter. His explanation used a lot of higher mathematics, and it was soon obvious that the only people who could understand him were Doil, Frank, the silent Filio, and Mani, who said that though she understood nothing about machinery, the concepts Isnek spoke of were like the mathematics that she practised at home.

"This is all very well," said Tenkle impatiently. "But what I want to know is how long it will take us to get home. How many hours?"

"My dear man, we're talking about *days*."

"Days? But I want to get out of here."

"So do we all, but I can't hurry it up, unless you know a way of speeding up the Galaxy. We've got to wait until the two suns are correctly aligned."

Tenkle smacked his hands together and walked away. "I can stalk and hunt and fight. But doing nothing is no good. No good at all."

"How about exploring the storage area up there?" Valerie suggested. "You could make a list of everything useful you find. Then if we should need something in a hurry..."

Tenkle brightened and he swung up the spiral staircase. Soon they could hear his footsteps on the ceiling above the living room. After a few minutes Sturpis followed him.

I wish it were as simple to keep Susan happy, thought Valerie with a sigh. "I want to go home." And two minutes later: "Valerie, take me home *now*." It's not her fault, poor dear, she told herself firmly as she tried to explain without snapping. She's been imprisoned and doped and scared half to death.

Valerie's head was beginning to ache. She forced a smile. "Come on, love. Help me get lunch. We've got to keep everyone fed and ourselves occupied, or we'll go squirrelly waiting for something to happen."

There were a few accidents on the way to preparing a hot meal; after all, it wasn't easy using an alien stove and opening alien cans of food, but when it was done she was quite proud of herself and her small helper. She called the preoccupied scientists from the console.

"How's it going anyway?"

"We're beginning to get the hang of the instruments," Doil told her. "It's a problem dealing with an alien mind. What seems obvious to us isn't to them and vice versa. You can't take anything for granted."

"You should try linking up with Fifth Daughter. I bet she could help, the way she helped me find the log book. I know you don't understand maths, Fifth Daughter, but I bet if they explain to you what they think they find as they go along, you could make a guess as to how the popeyes would have used it. It's like one race going with the wheel and another with the lever, if you see what I mean."

"Illogical but interesting," pronounced Isnek Ansnek.

"All right, Fifth Daughter, you're part of the team as soon as we're through with this excellent meal. Valerie, we'll need you too. We've found a table that we think has the times of maximum power when the Transmitter can be used. It certainly has something to do with the relationship of this spot on the planet to the tensions and forces between the two suns. So much we know, but we must know the exact times of transmission."

"I don't know many astronomical words. After all, Dr Mushni was a linguist. But I'll try."

"You're our only chance, Val. Otherwise we're just guessing," Frank said earnestly, and she nearly burst with pride.

But what a responsibility, she thought later, as she struggled with unfamiliar words and figures and the others continued their work at the console. Sturpis and Tenkle, the men of action, were left to entertain Susan.

"But what are we going to *do* with her?"

"If two grown men can't look after one little girl . . ." she said, her finger on the line she was working with, and looked up to see Frank's grin. "Well," she said defensively, and then grinned back.

Halfway through the afternoon she had an inspiration. "Mr Ansnek?"

"You have found the answer."

"Not quite, but I think I've got the code. You recall everything important you've seen, don't you?"

"Yes, indeed."

"Thank goodness! Will you write down the dates and

times that were in the first column of the logbook of arrivals at the Transmitter. If I can compare them with what I've done here I should know if I'm on the right track."

"Of course. How foolish of me not to have thought of it myself!" He rapidly produced a neat column of figures.

It worked. After two guesses the third was right on. The times meshed perfectly. Now she had the missing terms and could read the book perfectly. She could read into the future, *their* future, and tell the others exactly when they could escape. If the others really understood how the Matter Transmitter worked, that was.

She counted over on her fingers twice to be on the safe side. Then she compared her findings with the digital clock set centrally above the instrument panel.

"Tomorrow at fourteen twenty-three," she told them triumphantly. She thought they would be delighted with her, but their faces fell.

"Tomorrow?"

"So soon! We'll never understand it all by then."

"You can *try*, can't you?"

"Sure we can, but ... well, when's the next chance after that?"

Valerie went back to her tables and did some more calculations. She might never understand astrophysics, but thank goodness there was nothing wrong with her arithmetic.

"The day after that. Soon after sunrise. Oh-eight-twelve. And you'd jolly well better be ready by then," she went on as Frank's mouth opened. "Because the next 'window' isn't for absolutely ages and they'll have turned off the water and starved us out by then. So we'd better get it right by tomorrow, or the next day at the very latest."

They had a filling but hurried supper, and, except for

Susan, who was tucked up in one of the bunks and told a long bedtime story, nobody thought of sleep.

Tenkle's and Sturpis's list of stores was gone over and a box of spare parts was laid out on the dining room table. Here again, Fifth Daughter's intuition combined with Isnek Ansnek's experience had to take the place of actual knowledge. But by the time night was over and the light of the distant sun was sending a pale gleam through the dome of the Tower, they had a pretty solid idea of how everything worked. "Though we'll never know for sure until we try," Frank said with a worried sigh.

They cut a piece of sheet copper and Tenkle and Donald between them set up an engraving tool and wrote a message, which was the end result of a precious hour spent in argument.

Tenkle had wanted to have a volunteer test out the machine, with himself leading the way. "It's the only way to be sure."

Filio and Sturpis had agreed with him.

Mani stated the feelings of the others. "I would be most happy to sacrifice my life to ensure the safe return of the rest. But I would not want it to be wasted, that is foolish. I think we should send a message first."

"Suppose whoever picks it up doesn't understand it?"

"If they can't read Intergalactic they're not members of the Federation, and perhaps we might not wish to transmit ourselves there."

"Out of the frying pan into the fire," said Valerie helpfully, which had to be explained to Isnek Ansnek, wasting more precious time.

Then they had to agree on the wording of the message. In the end Frank engraved in Intergalactic Common Speech:

Friendly Mission from Eden, Persis, Tabara, Nahkan, Plabzkitza and Japonica. May we transmit safely to this

place? Please respond immediately with planet name
and coordinates.

The message was headed with the Federation Peace
Symbol, recognised and honoured by seven-tenths of the
known planets in the Milky Way Galaxy.

"It looks terrific, Frank."

"It certainly inspires confidence."

"Let's hope it's not picked up by some native on a
primitive planet and used as a juju symbol."

They stared blankly at Tenkle from whom this depress-
ing idea had come.

"Perhaps we ought to have a duplicate. Just in case we
don't get it back."

Frank groaned and flexed his cramped fingers.

"How long do we have at that first 'window', Val?"
Doil asked.

"About thirty-eight minutes."

"There's time. Let's make a second message plate, just in
case. Sorry, Frank."

"All right. But it's not going to look as classy as the first
one, I can tell you. I'm getting writer's cramp."

The numbers on the digital clock turned slowly over. Frank
took the first copper plate and laid it carefully in the precise
centre of the metal cage. Isnek Ansnek pulled a lever and the
roof slowly slid apart, so that a slit of blue sky showed
between the plastic halves of the dome. Doil ran up the spiral
staircase to the platform under the dome where the focusing
mechanism for the lens was placed. He moved the controls.

"Stop. That's it." Frank shouted up the tower and Doil's
voice echoed hollowly back in acknowledgement.

"What are we aiming for?" Valerie asked.

"I can point to it on the popeyes' star chart, but what it's
Federation name is, and if it's a Federation planet, I
haven't a clue. We're guessing. We just picked a planet

that's fairly near and in a good position for this transmission time."

"Let's pray this works." Valerie squeezed Susan's hand. They stood outside the cage, staring at the precious piece of copper. The clock moved forward.

14:20, 14:21, 14:22.

"Get ready. Now!"

Isnek and Frank busied themselves at the controls.

"Nothing's working."

"Come on. We can't be that far wrong!"

Fifth Daughter touched Valerie and she shouted to the others. "The gate. How stupid. It's got to be shut before anything will work. Quick, someone, help." She pushed the right half and Sturpis grabbed the left. The gates joined and clicked. The locking bar fell into place and the copper plate winked out of sight.

"We've done it!"

"Yeah!"

"Good lord, it works!"

After the initial excitement they all calmed down and their eyes went from the empty floor of the cage to the clock above the console and back again.

"Come on, someone, pick it up," Frank said under his breath.

14:28, 14:29, 14:30...

"How long before we give up and try another planet?"

"Eight more minutes."

"Eight!"

They watched and waited.

At the top of the spiral staircase Doil watched the dials unblinkingly, keeping the lens focused on one tiny spot on an unknown planet, while both of them turned about their separate suns. It was like a life-line. Someone had to have hold of both ends for it to work. And it was the lens that did all the holding.

"Fourteen thirty-nine. Valerie, are you ready with the second plate if we need it? Get ready to change focus, Doil."

"Hang on. I'm getting a reading. The plate's been moved. Hold it...Now! Transmit back."

"There it is," Valerie shouted.

The plate was in the cage, and on it rested a huge flower, an exotic shape of flame and purple with a heart like creamy velvet. Its scent filled the room.

Valerie slid back the bolt and pulled open one side of the door. She ran in, grabbed the plate and flower and ran out again.

Frank snatched the plate from her and stared at it. He turned it over. His hand dropped. "Nothing."

For an instant no one took the news in.

"The flower," Valerie held it out in her cupped hands. "Someone put it there, didn't they? It was cut. It didn't fall."

"Don't you see, Val? It's a primitive 'hands-off' culture. The flower is an offering to the unknown. It might be a beautiful place, but the people there could never help us get *home*."

"But..." Valerie blinked tears from her eyes.

"It's no *good*, Val." Frank shook her gently and she nodded.

"Next try, Doil," Isnek shouted up and went back to the console.

Frank ran into the cage to replace the plate. This time he wasn't fussy about it. He just dropped it and ran out. "Ready!"

They swung the gate shut.

"On target." Doil's voice echoed eerily down from the top of the tower.

"Here we go then." The plate vanished. "Fourteen forty-one. How long do we have left, Val?"

"Fifteen minutes, that's all." Valerie saw Susan looking anxiously at her face, and she managed a smile. "It'll be all right. You see."

They watched the clock. The instruments. The floor of the cage.

14:42 ... 14:43 ...

Valerie held the flower. The creamy centre was faintly hairy, each hair surmounted by a drop of sweet smelling nectar. She stroked a crimson petal, wondering whose hand had cut it from the plant and laid it gently on the copper plate. What must they have thought when it vanished again? "Can I have it, Val, *please*." Susan tugged her arm. She gave her the flower and concentrated on the clock.

14:51 ...

Seventy percent of the known planets are members of the Federation. Seventy percent.

14:52 ...

"I'm getting a reading. Be ready to switch to 'receive' ... Now!"

"There it is!" Valerie swung open the door and bent over the plate. "I think..." She straightened up and stared as if she couldn't believe it. "It has. It's got writing on it!"

She held it up to the light, deciphering the hasty scratch marks. "Hagerdorn. 23.001. 148.920, 97.368. Welcome and good luck."

"We've done it!"

"Lock onto those co-ordinates, Doil," Frank shouted up. "Don't let them go."

"Locked in," the disembodied voice floated down.

The life-line, thought Valerie. Could it really survive the swinging orbit of each of their planets around its own sun? Would the line really still be there tomorrow?

"Hagerdorn," Frank told Doil as he ran down the spiral staircase. "I just wish we had Blackie's Register of Planets..."

"You won't need it." Doil's grin spread across his face. "I know it. It's hardly two parsecs from Tabara. Why, my wife's from Hagerdorn, man!"

No wonder he was all smiles, thought Valerie. Like going home. But so it was for all of them. Hagerdorn was a Federation planet. By this time tomorrow, if all goes well, we'll be there. We'll have phoned Mum and Dad. This time *tomorrow*. She hugged Susan. "Do you understand? We're going home. Really truly going home!"

Doil took charge. "...still have to work out the maximum load we dare send at a time. The length of time at the next window—Valerie, you get on with that. The order in which we transport." He hesitated, looking from face to face. "Fifth Daughter, you and Mani must do your best to make up a list. And we need one more good meal. Then we'll sleep in shifts, four hours each, three shifts. That'll give us enough time."

Now at last the hours flew by. Mani and Fifth Daughter came up with their list, which was unarguable. Since Doil was married to a Hagerdorner and knew the planet he was to go first together with Tenkle and Susan. It was felt that her appearance with them would quieten any fears that the transmission was some kind of invasion. Doil would have liked to stay to the last, since he knew more about the Transmitter than any of them except Isnek, but they all agreed that for him to go first would be the safest for them all.

Sturpis and Filio were to follow with Mani and Fifth Daughter after the two humanoids. Last were to be Frank, Valerie and Isnek, mostly because Valerie and Isnek each weighed under fifty kilograms and could go together without overloading the Transmitter. That last transmission was going to be the difficult one. It would take split second timing if it was going to work.

Doil, Frank, Mani and Fifth Daughter slept first, while

Valerie and Tenkle made a big dinner — Sturpis' and Filio's idea of food was too weird to leave them in charge. Valerie was to sleep next, with Susan and Tenkle.

Sleep, she thought restlessly, after she'd lifted Susan up into the high bed and climbed up after her. I'm far too excited ever to *sleep*. But to her surprise the next thing she knew was Mani shaking her shoulder. She slipped quietly out of the room, determined to let Susan sleep until the last possible moment.

The Tower bustled with activity. Less than five hours to go! While she had been sleeping, Doil, Frank and Isnek had rigged a relay from the lens mechanism to the control panel, so that no one would have to remain on the platform during the transmission. Their final concern was to wire in a delay device so that the last group could leave safely. Valerie feverishly rechecked her times.

Seven-fifty. Valerie went to waken Sturpis and Filio and Susan, who woke up grouchy. "Come on, smile. We're going home. You first of all." She hugged her.

By eight everyone was ready beside the console.

"Remember to leave a message as soon as you've arrived. I'll reverse the field in one minute. For goodness' sake get out of the way and warn everyone else off. We don't want to be transmitting people back in here by mistake. There's no spare time for errors."

"What if we land in water?" Valerie asked suddenly.

"We won't." Doil was confident. "The copper plate was safe. We will be too. We can count on the coordinates."

8:10 . . . Doil and Tenkle went into the cage. Valerie kissed Susan and pushed her gently in. Doil and Tenkle took her hands, but Susan's lip trembled as the door slammed shut. Valerie knelt outside, her face against the bars. "It's all right. Frank and I'll be with you in a couple of minutes. And it'll be nice. Parties and real food."

"Ice cream?"

"Yes, of course."

"Promise?"

"I promise."

8:12.

"Goodbye."

"Good luck!"

Doil, Tenkle and Susan vanished with a shimmer like desert heat.

8:13 ... A hair ribbon appeared, tied to a scrap of paper.

Valerie grabbed it and unfolded the paper. "It says: OK. Oh, Frank, they're safe. Susan's safe!"

Frank's smile was wide as he turned to Sturpis and Filio. "Your turn now, in you go."

"You good people." Sturpis rushed around hugging everyone.

"Go on. No time for that now. See you soon."

8:15 ... As the two bear-like humanoids vanished, Fifth Daughter gave a terrible cry and fell to the ground.

"What is it? Are you hurt?" Valerie knelt beside her. "Oh, what's happened?" She tried to lift the large pink humanoid, but as soon as she touched her she too cried out in pain. "Oh, Frank, Moab's dying. It's held back the popeyes all this time in spite of their flamethrowers. But now they're using some horrible acid ... oh!" She wept, her arms around Fifth Daughter.

8:18.

"Valerie, pull yourself together. Come on. Get up. You've got to get Fifth Daughter into the cage. We're losing time." Frank's voice was urgent.

She scrambled to her feet and with Mani's help tried to pull Fifth Daughter up, but her weight was too much for them.

"Fifth Daughter, we need you to find Moab's planet. You're going to have to plant its seeds, so it won't be dead any more. You can do it. You'll feel the right place. Go to Susan and get the seeds from her *now*."

Only then would Fifth Daughter allow them to help her into the cage. Valerie left her and Mani and ran out to shut the door.

8.20...Frank moved the dial and they were gone.

Valerie leaned against the cage door. She felt sick and shaken at the overflow from Fifth Daughter's mind of the last agony of Moab as the popeyes sprayed the turf with corrosive, burned the roots of the trees. Metre by metre they had eaten Moab away, and now nothing stood between the popeyes and the Tower.

Frank and Isnek were bent over the console, wiring in the remote control device. "Do not hurry," Isnek cautioned Frank. "A bad connection might leave us stranded here, or locked in space for ever as a stream of disconnected electrons. There is enough time."

"How much?" asked Frank between his teeth. "Val, how much time?"

Valerie looked at the clock. 18:27... "Don't worry, Frank. Almost seven minutes left." She forced her voice to sound cheerful. "Lots of time." Her palms were sweating and she rubbed them against her jumpsuit, and clenched her fists. She willed Isnek and Frank to get on with it. Hurry. Hurry...

18:28...The 'window' closed at 8:34, forever, as far as they were concerned. The popeyes would force the door, blow it up...oh, hurry!

18:29...Frank wiped the sweat out of his eyes and blinked. "Let's send Valerie on ahead."

"No way, Frank. It'll waste precious time. We go together or not at all." The heroic words came out of her mouth without her meaning them in the least. She wanted desperately to run inside the cage and beg them to transmit her to Hagerdorn right *now*.

There was a thundering noise outside and the door shook. Frank dropped his soldering iron, swore and bent to pick it up.

"It's all right, Frank. I have the last connections. All complete." Isnek's voice was quietly satisfied. "Two minutes left, but I estimate that the door will go sooner. Into the cage quickly, while I switch over." He pushed Frank and Valerie into the cage and carefully pulled out a pair of wires. The door slammed and he made the final connection. There was a sudden spark...

Valerie no longer felt Frank's hand in hers, no longer felt the weight of her feet on the ground, nor the air stale and smoky in her lungs. She would have opened her mouth to scream, but she had no mouth, no throat, no breath.

11

Hagerdorn

The electrons, atoms, molecules, the flesh and bone and skin and hair that were Valerie all came together again and tumbled to the ground. She wriggled her toes and felt that they belonged to her. She could feel Frank's hand reassuringly warm in hers, and, when she squeezed it, it squeezed back. She opened her eyes cautiously, wondering what in the Galaxy she would see.

Soft sky and a single G-type sun. She sat up and took a deep breath. A meadow of sweet-smelling grass sloped gently down to a brook winding across a valley bottom. Willow trees dropped over their reflections and large gold and grey birds floated serenely down on the current. On the far side paths led up to the city wall. Above its jade-coloured heights, turrets, spires and walkways were balanced in a confusion of bright colour up, up, almost to the clouds. Still dazed, she watched a stream of people beginning to leave the city, coming down the hill to meet them.

She was pulled to her feet and dragged away from the grassy spot where she had been sitting. And there were the others! Susan . . . she ran and hugged her. Dear Fifth Daughter and Mani. Tenkle gruffly pleased to see her, shaking her hand most painfully. The two humanoids, Sturpis and Filio. And Isnek, standing alone, a little dazed, still holding in his right hand the remains of the connection that had brought them safely through.

"I can't believe it, Isnek, I didn't think you'd made it. Oh, I could kiss you!"

Isnek Ansnek drew hastily back. "There is no need, I assure you. I have told you twice before: my safety is the first imperative. And you've started crying again — oh, do watch out!"

Valerie's tears turned to giggles. "I'm sorry. I forgot. Well, you won't have to worry about rust any more. You'll be able to have your re-fit. Think of it, Mr Ansnek."

"I am. Indeed I am. Doil has told me that the Hagerdorners are expert craftspeople. I shall be a new man."

By now the people from the city had begun to cross the brook. Doil walked quickly down to meet a man with an imposing chain around his neck. They shook hands and Doil talked rapidly. The man turned and held up his arms to the oncoming crowd.

"Keep back," he warned them. "The Matter Transmitter is probably still operating. It could reverse at any time. This area is a danger to us all."

"I wish we had a way of neutralising it for ever," Doil said.

"And the popeyes," Tenkle added grimly.

"Oh, no, Tenkle." Valerie shivered. "That would make us as bad as them. I know they were awful — that basement room and the Zoo and everything. But maybe it wasn't all their fault. Maybe being stuck behind that obscuring cloud being ignored by everyone helped make them the way they are."

"Well, just listen to you, Val. Perhaps you'd better think about joining the Federation Team that goes in to re-educate them, once we've located their planet."

"Maybe I just will." Valerie stuck her chin up.

Frank thumped her on the back. "Do you know, I believe you could, big sister. Come on. Let's all go up to the city and find out how quickly we can get an interplanetary call through to Eden. I bet it won't be long before they've got us through to Mother and Father." He swung Susan onto his shoulders with a grunt. "When I gave you a ride out to the thorn bush back on DeePeeThree you weighed about ten kilograms less."

"Yes, really Susan, you're going to have to go on a diet. The widow Karosh must have really stuffed you."

"But it was horrid food and you *promised* me ice-cream, Val. You know you did."

"All right. Ice-cream first and *then* a diet."

Frank and Valerie walked across a rustic bridge, Susan bumping up and down on Frank's shoulders. Above them the city glowed like a huge many-faceted jewel. Gossamer-light flyers swooped like birds between the spires. There was the sound of music and singing and people waiting at the gate to greet them with flowers. It was almost as beautiful as Eden. The memory of life on the popeye world began to fade like a bad dream.

But Valerie sighed. "One thing really bothers me, Frank."

"What's that?"

"When we *do* find the popeye world, what do you suppose the Federation will do with the Matter Trans-mitter?"

"Use it, of course. What else? It'll be an incredible advance for civilization. It's the dream that scientists have sought after ever since Bill Enroy vanished all those centur-ies ago and his notes with him."

"Will Hagerdorn be any the better off? Or Eden?"

"It's progress," said Frank definitely. "And you can't stop progress."

What really *is* progress? Valerie wondered as they walked under the archway of the great gate. She compared the people of Hagerdorn and Eden and other planets she'd visited, with the horrible selfish lazy popeyes. Had they always been that horrid? Or maybe it had started when they stole the Matter Transmitter from Bill Enroy. Maybe, little by little, having the Matter Transmitter had made them as nasty as they were today. Having a machine like that meant that you could grab more easily than you could give.

Well, there wasn't much she could do about it right now, except talk to Mother and Father about how she felt. And then work hard at growing up herself, so that maybe one day she could be part of the decisions.